DATE DUE

Sli

Advance Praise for *YaYa & YoYo: Sliding Into the New Year*

"I feel like I just began the journey of *YaYa and YoYo* and am looking forward to their next adventures. I found myself smiling while I read. YaYa's voice as a Jewish fifth-grader gives many children an opportunity to see themselves in the characters of this book and feel a sense of belonging. We have waited a long time for a series like this one!"

Jane Taubenfeld Cohen
Head of School, South Area Solomon Schechter Day School
Author of *We Can Make It Happen!*

"*YaYa & YoYo: Sliding Into the New Year* is just the sort of wonderful and entertaining story I wish was around when my children were young. It is an organic and engaging way to teach both Jews and non-Jews about the transforming power of the central Jewish holiday of Rosh Hashanah. Weinstein does something so rare—she captures with such honesty and groundedness a healthy family unafraid of emotion and intimacy."

Rabbi Irwin Kula
President, CLAL (The National Jewish Center for Learning and Leadership)
Author of *Yearnings: Embracing the Sacred Messiness of Life*

"In *Sliding Into the New Year*, Dori Weinstein captures the attention of youngsters and their parents alike with captivating storytelling that links contemporary kids, their families, and their lives to the core of Jewish traditions and values. In this first book in the series, YaYa's and YoYo's adventures create wonderful opportunities for parents and children to engage in meaningful Jewish discussions about issues that might well have emerged from their own family experiences."

Rabbi Alvin Mars, Ph.D.
Sr. Consultant to the President of the JCC Association of North America
for Education Development

"It is so refreshing to find a Jewish book for tweens and pre-teens that is current, relevant and relatable. Ellie, Joel and the whole Silver clan are likable and funny. Kids will learn about the holiday of Rosh Hashanah in a new and engaging way. Thank you, Dori, for bringing this series to us!"

Gila Hadani Ward
Director of Lifelong Learning at Temple Beth Sholom
Roslyn Heights, NY

"Finally, a Jewish book for young readers that is well-written, engaging, lots of fun, and has important lessons to teach. I love it. And the best of all, it is the first in a series."

Rabbi Kerry M. Olitzky
Executive Director, Jewish Outreach Institute
Author of *The Complete How To Handbook for Jewish Living*

"A delightful and engaging story of growth into young adulthood and the challenges of faith. A wonderful opportunity for parents and children to explore together the meaning of the High Holy Days."

Rabbi Steven Wernick
Executive VP, United Synagogue of Conservative Judaism

"*YaYa & YoYo: Sliding Into the New Year* is not only a pleasure to read, but also paves the way for a captivating Jewish journey for kids and pre-teens. Dori Weinstein uses humor, wisdom and warmth to address the challenges that every Jewish family faces in raising committed, knowledgeable Jews in the 21st century. I am sure that YaYa and YoYo are going to become household names in the vital enterprise of strengthening Jewish identity and commitment. My kids and I can't wait to hear about their next adventures!"

Rabbi Charles Savenor
Executive Director, Metropolitan New York District
United Synagogue of Conservative Judaism

"As Adam Sandler's Chanukah songs prove, we like to know that we're not alone, even though we're members of a minority religion. In *YaYa & YoYo*, Jewish children will find fictional characters who inhabit the same world, use the same words, and face the same woes as they do. Dori Weinstein's first book is a testament to her love of Judaism, family, and teaching!"

Sari Steinberg
Author of *...And Then There Were Dinosaurs*
and *King Solomon Figures It Out*

"Finally, a book that is 'teachy' without being preachy. Dori Weinstein knows and respects her audience. By writing enjoyable, credible and intelligent fiction, she shows that learning and fun are not mutually exclusive. In fact, the subject of this book is one that parents and children can have a substantive discussion about together.

Rabbi Hayim Herring, PhD
Executive Director, STAR (Synagogues: Transformation and Renewal)
President and CEO, Herring Consulting Network

"'Finding who I am' is every young person's struggle, and adding Jewish identity to the mix makes the challenge all the more difficult. Dori Weinstein takes readers on this journey in a delightful way with a conclusion that is hard to predict. The interplay between the characters is realistic and entertaining. A great read for kids and pre-teens!"

Gil Mann
Author of *How to Get More Out of Being Jewish Even if... A. You are not sure you believe in God, B. You think going to synagogue is a waste of time, C. You think keeping kosher is stupid, D. You hated Hebrew school, or E All of the above!*

YaYa & YoYo

Sliding Into the New Year

Dori Weinstein

Yaldah Publishing
St. Paul

YAYA & YOYO: SLIDING INTO THE NEW YEAR. Text copyright © 2011 by Dori Weinstein. All rights reserved. Printed in the United States of America on acid-free paper. First edition. No part of this book may be reproduced, scanned, or distributed in any printed or electronic form without written permission from the publisher except in the case of brief quotations embodied in critical articles or reviews. For information, address Yaldah Publishing, PO Box 18662, Saint Paul, MN, 55118. www.yaldahpublishing.com.

The yud-lamed logo is a registered trademark of Yaldah Publishing.

While every effort has been made to provide accurate Internet addresses at the time of publication, neither the publisher nor the author assume any responsibility for errors, or for changes that occur after publication. Further, the publisher does not have any control over and does not assume any responsibility for author or third-party websites or their content.

Cover illustration © by Martha Rast
Editor: Leslie Martin

Publisher's Cataloging-in-Publication data

Weinstein, Dori.
    Sliding into the new year / by Dori Weinstein.
    p. cm.
    ISBN 978-1-59287-201-5 (pbk)
    ISBN 978-1-59287-301-2 (ebook)
    Series : YaYa & YoYo, 1.
    Summary : Fifth-grader Ellie Silver (YaYa) plans to visit a water park with her friend until her twin, Joel (YoYo), tells her it conflicts with Rosh Hashanah.

    1. Rosh ha-Shanah--Juvenile fiction. 2. Jews--United States--Juvenile fiction. 3. Fasts and feasts--Judaism--Juvenile fiction. 4. Twins--Juvenile fiction. 5. Families --Juvenile fiction. I. Series. II. Title.

PZ7.W43667 Sli 2010
[Fic] –dd22   2010939693

9   8   7   6   5   4   3   2   1

In memory of my mom

Sandra Alexander Margolin

*who taught me to love words, language and my heritage
(and mint chocolate chip ice cream!)*

Contents

ﭏ 1

Morning Rush Hour

The knot in my hair was as big as a watermelon. Well, more like a cantaloupe. A matzah ball? Okay, fine, it was the size of an olive. An olive that had the pit taken out of it . . . and that someone had bitten in half . . . and was a little bit shriveled up. But it was a bad one. It became a battle between me and the hairy beast and I was planning to win.

I was standing in front of the bathroom mirror trying to force the teeth of my comb through the clump of hair when my brother Joel yelled to me from the front door. "Come on, YaYa, we're going to be late for school!"

My name is Ellie Silver, but YaYa is my family nickname because my Hebrew name is Yael (it's pronounced Ya-el, rhymes with "Ma Bell"). Joel's Hebrew name is Yoel (rhymes with "toe smell").

My parents thought it would be cute to have twins named Yael and Yoel. I know, it's totally corny, but since we usually go by our English names, most people don't even realize that our names go together at all.

To make things even more dorky, when we were babies, Joel called me YaYa and somehow our corny names morphed into even cornier nicknames. Even now, at almost eleven years old, we are still called YaYa and YoYo. Luckily, hardly anybody outside of our family knows about this. Our nicknames have become almost like a secret handshake between us, and we actually do like using them with one another—as long as no one else hears.

I stuck my head out of the bathroom and called, "I'm coming, I'm coming. Chill out, Little Bro." I know he hates it when I call him that, but I can't stand it when he rushes me.

"I'm not your 'Little Bro.' Quit calling me that!" he shouted, sounding impatient. We've been having this argument for as long as I can remember.

"Are too!" I said through gritted teeth, still fighting the knot in a fistful of hair. "I'm a whole . . . day . . . older . . . and you . . . know it." The hairy beast was winning. I needed a different strategy with stronger ammunition: I switched to my heavy-duty wire-bristle hairbrush.

"Not a whole day, thirteen minutes! And that was most definitely the last time you were ever ready to leave before me."

I couldn't argue with him there. But I really am a whole day older than him. My birthday is on October eighth and his is on the ninth. I was born at five minutes before midnight. He didn't show up until eight minutes *after* midnight, the next day. True, it is only thirteen minutes, but my birthday is a day before his. I have framed copies of our birth certificates on the wall over my bed to prove it.

I turned back to the mirror for one last battle with my hair. While looking in the mirror, I noticed that the freckles that had popped up on my cheeks over the summer were starting to fade. One of my favorite things about being outside at Camp Shemesh, the day camp Joel and I go to, is that I always get my "summer face," as I like to call it. It's not fair—Joel gets to keep his freckles all year long. Mine only show up for a couple of months, like relatives that come to visit once a year.

At least I like my hair—that is, when it isn't all knotted up like a kite caught in a tree. It's just thick enough for me to braid easily and is a cool shade of light brown with blonde streaks in it. It gets a little bit darker in the winter, but it never gets as dark as Joel's. His is plain old boring brown. But his freckles make his face sort of interesting to look at. Mine do, too, even if it's just for a little while. But now they were leaving, just as I suspected Joel was about to do.

"Mom!" I yelled so she'd hear me downstairs, "have you seen my pink baseball cap?" So much for my great-looking hair. Once again, it was destined to end up hidden under a hat.

"Here, cover up your mop with this instead." Jeremy, my twelve-and-a-half- year-old brother, pulled his grungy old skateboard beanie off his head and tossed it to me as he passed by the bathroom doorway. It was an old gray knit hat that looked like it had never been washed and smelled like a cross between stinky socks and hair gel. And maybe something else I couldn't quite make out. Garlic? Wet dog?

"Gross!" I said. "I don't want to wear this hideous thing!" I picked it up between my thumb and forefinger, careful not to let any other part of my hand touch it, and flung it back at him.

"Ever heard of 'thanks?'" he grumbled as he fitted it back on his head.

"Yeah. Thanks, but no thanks," I said with a shudder as he headed down the stairs.

Mom called up to me. "Why don't you wear your Niagara Falls hat?"

"Lost it sometime last week," I replied, putting the hairbrush away and pulling out an elastic band for my hair. I was so sad that I lost that hat. We had just bought it on a family trip in June and it was my new favorite hat.

"Oh, YaYa, you lost it already? That's too bad," Mom said, sounding disappointed but not particularly surprised. I could just picture the maybe-if-you-cleaned-your-room-once-in-a-while-you-wouldn't-lose-things look on her face. "Well, I think I saw the pink one somewhere near your bookshelf." I appreciated her holding back on her "clean your room" lecture. No time for that now!

"Bookshelf. Thanks." I ran down the hall toward my bedroom. On my way, I glanced inside Joel's uncluttered room. I saw his neatly made bed, but I didn't see my hat in there. Big surprise.

I headed straight to my bookshelf and spotted the pink brim. It was sticking out from under a stack of board games, stuffed animals, and books. I carefully slipped the hat out, trying not to topple the wobbly tower. The whole thing came tumbling down anyway, but I didn't have time to pick it all up. So I just left everything in a heap on the floor, pulled my hair back into a ponytail, and put on my baseball cap. I ran out of my room and back down the hall. I reached the top of the stairs in time to see Joel rolling his eyes at me.

"See ya," he said to Dad, who was at his computer in the office by the front door. He gave Mom a kiss on the cheek, called, "'Bye, Mom, love you," over his shoulder, and started walking down the driveway . . . without me.

I flew down the stairs and rushed into the kitchen. Jeremy was sitting at the table, eating a bowl of corn flakes. Chances are, it was already his fourth serving. It seems that lately, no matter how much food is in front of him, he never gets full. My mom says he has a bottomless pit for a stomach.

Jeremy just started seventh grade at Harrison Junior High School. He walks, bikes, or skateboards to school and doesn't have to leave as early as we do. So, every morning while I'm bouncing around from one thing to the next, like the ball inside a pinball machine, he just hangs out at the table, reads something, and eats. And eats. And eats some more. It's like he's on vacation at the beach, with nowhere to go and nothing to worry about.

Jeremy was leaning over his breakfast, reading the sports section of the newspaper, not even looking down to see if his spoon was actually dipping into the bowl. He was staring intently at the newspaper with his spoon moving automatically from the bowl to his mouth and back to the bowl again.

Nowadays, Jeremy seems to think he's too cool to be with me or Joel. Jeremy and I always used to get along really well. That is, until he came back from sleep-away camp this summer. Now he acts like he has much more important things to do than talk to us lowly fifth-graders. He's getting ready for his bar mitzvah, which will be in February, and I guess that makes him feel much older and more grown-up than us. He's all wrapped up in his own little world. I'd even go so far as to say he's been downright rude. Mom says it's a phase and it will pass, but I'm not so sure I can live through it for much longer.

Every now and then, he'll forget about his "Mr. Cool" act and come to our rooms to hang out with us or invite us to play video games with him just like the old days. But those times seem to be happening less and less. At breakfast (or "feeding time," as I like to call it), he completely ignores everyone and everything around him.

"See you later, Jay," I said, hoping for some sign of life.

I thought I heard a grunt.

Jeremy's family nickname is JayJay, or sometimes, just Jay. When we got our "cute little nicknames" we were about a year old. Jeremy was three and of course he didn't want to be left out. He wanted a cute little nickname like we had, and insisted on being called by his Hebrew name, too. Well, since his name is Yeremeeyahu, calling him YerYer was just plain weird. I mean, what kind of a name is YerYer? YaYa and YoYo may be goofy names, but YerYer just sounds ridiculous!

Our dad convinced Jeremy that YerYer wasn't such a great idea. As a salesman, Dad has a special talent for getting people to listen to him, and he somehow convinced Jeremy that JayJay was a better nickname than YerYer. Now he's all, "I'm in junior high. I'm so mature." So he started having the kids at school call him Jay instead of Jeremy. Personally, I think it'll take a lot more than changing his name to make him as cool as he thinks he is. Whatever . . .

I didn't have time to deal with Mr. Cool or his attitude. I had a bus to catch! I snatched what was left of my bagel, wrapped it in a napkin, slurped one last sip of orange juice, and raced to the door. "'Bye, Dad," I called as I ran past his office. "'Bye, Mom. See you later," I said as I grabbed my backpack and lunch box and blew her an air kiss.

"Have a great day at school, sweetie," Mom said in her bathrobe and slippers. She's an artist. She paints and does calligraphy and other stuff in her studio up in the attic. Unless she's off to an art show or meeting with a client, she doesn't have to rush out the door in the morning like the rest of us. Lucky!

My hand was on the doorknob and I had just about made it out the door when Mom stopped me in my tracks.

"Hold on, YaYa. Do you have your flute? You have band practice today."

Aargh! No, I did not have my flute. Was there any chance that I would actually make my bus on time?

And so began Wednesday. Another hectic, rushed, and stressful morning, just like all the others.

2

Indiana Ellie and Jokin' Joel

Last year Ms. Holmes, my fourth grade teacher, wrote in my report card, "Ellie needs to work on her organizational skills." I was really hoping that I'd get a fresh start and do better now that we're beginning a new school year. But here I am, two weeks into fifth grade, and I've already lost one sweatshirt and my favorite hat. And I forgot to bring my flute to school last week, too. Well, in my defense, it was only our first band practice, so I wasn't used to bringing it yet.

I hurried back upstairs to my room. Like an Olympic hurdle-jumper, I leaped over the mountain of board games that had spilled on the floor, kicked some stuffed animals out of the way, snatched the flute case from underneath a pile of papers, books and magazines on my desk, and ran back downstairs. Then I rushed out the door, which Mom was holding open for me. As I sped past her, I imagined that if we had been in a cartoon I would have left Mom spinning in a cloud of dust with papers flying all around.

I had to sprint all the way up the block to the corner where the school bus picks us up. Sure enough, I could see the flashing red lights. Joel was nowhere to be seen. He had already found a seat on the bus. Haley Walters, the only other kid who gets picked up at our stop, was just placing her foot on the top step when I arrived at the open door.

"Good morning, Miss Ellie," Roy smiled at me. Roy has been our bus driver since Joel and I were in kindergarten. He looked down at his watch. "Ten seconds later than yesterday. You're slipping." He winked at me from under his cap.

"Forgot . . . my . . . flute," I panted. Then, as I caught my breath, I said, "Don't worry, I'll beat my time tomorrow. I promise." I tried to wink back at him. Only I'm not really good at winking, so it was more of a blink. Roy chuckled and told me to find a seat.

I went to my usual spot, the third seat on the right, next to the window. Joel sits in the back where they tell jokes and he tries out his new "material" with his friends. He takes joke books out of the library, gets jokes from the Internet and even makes some up. Once in a while, I have to admit, he is kind of funny.

On the other hand, I do not appreciate his sense of humor when he makes me the butt of his jokes. Just last week he pulled another one on me. Mom lets me keep some of my friends' phone numbers on the speed-dial on our phone at home. Joel thought it would be funny if he switched all my numbers around. When I went to call my friend Camille, I got Megan; when I tried to call Abby, I found myself chatting with Jenna's mom. I was so confused until I saw him standing in the hallway, laughing as I hung up. I was ready to kill him!

The weird thing about Joel is that when he's not goofing around and telling jokes, or trying to pull a prank on me, he's usually learning about some new scientific stuff. One minute he'll act like a gross, disgusting, nearly eleven-year-old boy, putting fake vomit on the seat next to you (no kidding, he did that once). The next minute he'll be all serious as if he was a scientist in a white lab coat running chemical tests on a disgusting substance that *looks* like vomit. On the bus with his buddies, he's always clowning around and being a goofball. As long as I don't find a whoopee cushion—or something worse—in my seat, I really don't care what he does back there with his friends.

The boys were laughing and making noise in the back of the bus, but as I often do, I managed to tune it out as if I had an imaginary set of headphones on. I took out my math workbook and started doing the homework that I had forgotten about last night. Each morning I have about ten minutes from the time I get on the bus until my best friend Megan gets on. I rushed through my homework so we could hang out and talk before we got to school. Luckily, it was multiplying fractions and I'm really good at that, so it was a breeze. I finished just as Megan was coming down the aisle.

"Hey, Ellie," she said. "Can I sit with you or are you doing your homework again?"

"Nope, just finished," I told her as I slipped my workbook into my backpack.

"I have such amazing news!" she said as she sat down next to me. "I just found out that my cousins Michael and Lindsay from New York City are coming to town next weekend."

"Um, that's nice," I said, wondering what the big deal was. Her cousins came in pretty often.

"Well," she continued, "for some reason, their school is off on Monday and Tuesday. We have all sorts of family stuff that we're going to do together over the weekend, so they're going to stay until Tuesday morning."

"Okay," I said, waiting for the big news, so far not all that impressed by her newsflash.

"All right, Ellie Silver, tell me: What is the one place you're dying to go to? The one you haven't stopped talking about since the first time you saw the commercial for it on TV?"

I took a paper out of my backpack and rolled it up like a microphone. In my best announcer voice I recited word for word the TV commercial we've all heard about a hundred times this summer: "You mean, 'The newest, splashiest, wettest place this side of the Mississippi River, with some of the fastest waterslides in all of North America. Home of Terror Plummet and Dead Man's Drop. It could be none other than Splash World, America's newest and biggest indoor water park!'" I put down the pretend microphone. "Let me guess, you're taking Michael and Lindsay there?" I said, my voice getting higher, already feeling a little bit jealous.

Megan nodded. "I begged my parents to take us to Splash World before my cousins leave and they said yes! Not only won't we miss any school since we're going on Monday afternoon, but it's a weekday, so it won't be nearly as crowded as usual. Now, here's the best part. Are you ready?"

"That wasn't the best part?" I asked, sliding up to the edge of my seat, eager to hear where she was going with this.

"My mom said I could invite you to come, too! I was going to call you last night but decided that I wanted to tell you in person. Isn't that awesome?"

"No way! Are you serious? That is *so* cool! I'm *dying* to go to Splash World!" I pushed Megan's shoulder so hard that I almost knocked her off her seat.

"I know! This is going to be so great!" Megan said while straightening herself back into the seat. There isn't much that she doesn't know about me. Our mothers met when we were toddlers at a "Mommy and Me" class. Our moms are still friendly but that's mostly just because Megan and I have become such great friends. We met up again in kindergarten and have been, as we like to call ourselves, "best buds" ever since. Even though we aren't in the same class this year, we're still as close as ever. We have play dates and sleepovers all the time.

"Do you think your parents will let you go?" she asked. "I know it's a school night, but we'll be home early. Plus, Lindsay and Michael are leaving early in the morning, so we really can't stay too late. It'll be a short visit, but at least we'll get there."

"It sounds perfect. I can't imagine them saying no," I said. "Especially since it means that they don't have to go."

My parents are great and all, but they're not exactly into doing cool stuff like Megan's parents. They would never take me to a water park—at least not without my begging them until they couldn't stand it anymore (or promising to clean out the garage, mow the lawn, and do all the laundry every week for the rest of my life, which I actually considered until I came to my senses). My folks would rather take us to an art gallery or a history museum. It almost seems like if it isn't educational, it's a waste of time.

Despite all my pleading this summer, it never worked out to go to Splash World. Somehow, every weekend that we didn't already have plans was taken up by one of Mom and Dad's educational "field trips." And the one Sunday that could have possibly worked, Mom had to go wedding dress shopping with my Aunt Rachel.

As far as the "field trips" they take us on, I can usually deal with them, but it's not like I get all excited about going. Joel, on the other hand, really looks forward to these outings. He's much more like our parents that way.

Sometimes Mom and Dad call me "Indiana Ellie" after those old Indiana Jones adventure movies, because I'm the most daring one in the family, even more than Jeremy. Everyone at school calls my brother "Jokin' Joel," but if you asked me, I'd call him "Boring Boy." He may be a jokester, willing to risk telling a joke that won't get a laugh, but when it comes to trying something new and daring, he never wants to take chances or live on the edge.

Let me put it this way: if we were at a pool, I'd be doing flips off the high dive while he'd barely be putting one toe into the shallow end of the pool—wearing water wings! At an amusement park, you'd find me riding a hang down, inverted triple-loop roller coaster. Joel would be on the merry-go-round. With a seatbelt on. Tight. And he'd be gripping the pole so hard, you'd be able to see his knuckles sticking out and his palms would get all sweaty. Sometimes I wonder how it is that the two of us are twins.

Megan and I rode the rest of the way chatting non-stop about all the cool stuff we've heard about Splash World. The more we talked about it, the more excited I got. After all my efforts this summer, I couldn't believe I was actually going to go there!

Tamika Jones was sitting across the aisle from us and overheard our conversation (pretty hard not to hear us, since we were practically screaming!).

"I hear there's a new water-coaster that goes both up *and* down." Tamika said.

Dylan Cooper turned around in his seat in front of Tamika and said, "Yeah, it's true. I was there. It's awesome! And the Serpentine loops in and out of the building three different times."

"And that last drop makes you feel like little elves are tap-dancing inside of your stomach!" Stephanie Chun chimed in from two rows up.

Before long, there was a buzz of excitement in our little section at the front of the bus, with everyone chattering about Splash World and what they'd heard or done there. I felt the giddiness all the way down to my bones.

I threw my arms around Megan and gave her a huge, excited hug. This was going to be amazing! Megan and I promised each other that we'd go on the Tornado Twister together. She said that she would probably be too scared to go on Terror Plummet, but that she'd watch me. If I could, I'd have gone right then and there. I wished I didn't have to wait so long. Lindsay and Michael's visit couldn't come soon enough.

When we got to school, Megan stood up and said, "Okay, call me later. Ask your mom and let me know what she says."

"I will," I told her.

It wasn't until lunchtime that I realized I had left my flute on the bus.

3

Circuits and Slides

I couldn't concentrate most of the day. I was daydream-ing about sliding down Dead Man's Drop, Plungee Bun-gee and all the other mind-blowing water slides I've heard about at Splash World. Walking down the hall, I imagined I was flying down the slides so fast that everything around me looked blurry. I bumped into Ms. Russo, the art teach-er, on my way back from recess.

"Watch where you're going, dear," she said.

"Sorry," I replied. But even then, I couldn't snap out of it. My body may have been at Alexander Martin Elemen-tary School, but my head was definitely at the water park.

Finally, it was time for science, our last class of the day. I couldn't wait until school was over so I could tell Mom about Splash World. I walked into the science lab and lift-ed myself up onto my stool. I love that we get to use the lab now that we're in fifth grade. Only the fifth and sixth graders can use the lab. We get to do lots of cool hands-on science experiments and projects in there.

"Class," Mrs. Morris began, "today we are beginning our unit on electrical circuits. We will start by creating simple circuits together." She demonstrated how to connect everything to make the electricity flow through the wires and get the bulb to light up. "Once you have successfully gotten your bulb to light, you may experiment with more complex circuits. You can try to do a series circuit in which several bulbs are strung up together on a single circuit. Or perhaps you can figure out how to create a parallel circuit so that if one bulb goes out, the other ones stay on."

I glanced across the room over at Joel. He looked happier than if it was his birthday—almost as happy as I know I will look when I step foot in that water park.

Mrs. Morris continued, "I will come around to each table individually to see how you are doing. In the meantime, I will leave batteries, bulbs and wires up here on the table and you may come up to the front to collect your supplies."

I went to the front to get my materials and brought them back to my table. Even though we were supposed to hook up the wires to the bulb and the battery to make our simple circuits, I sort of got sidetracked. Instead, I twisted the wires around one another to make an imaginary super-scary slide. I was running my finger down the wire pretending that I was speeding down in a spray of water when Joel snuck up with his battery, bulb and wires and slid into the empty spot next to me. Mrs. Morris doesn't mind if we move around to work with different partners as long as we get our work done.

"Ahem," he cleared his throat, while organizing his equipment on the table. "What are you doing? You do realize that you can't get the bulb to light up if you don't connect the wire to the battery, don't you? You need to close the circuit in order to—"

"Yeah, I know, smarty pants," I snapped at him, sliding off my stool to reach the wires better. "I was just thinking about something else, that's all." I stood up a little straighter. I like that I'm almost an inch taller than him. Yeah, he's smart, kind of like a walking encyclopedia, but I am taller. And older. And I have better hair.

"Why would you be thinking about something else? This stuff is so cool!" he said. *Did he think that I couldn't see that he was standing on his tip-toes?*

"Yes, it is cool, but what I'm thinking about is even better."

"What could be better than building circuits?" he asked, completely serious. Then he got a far-off dreamy look on his face. "Well, I guess when we put switches in, that will be pretty awesome, but still—"

"Megan and her family are going to Splash World and they've invited me to come along," I interrupted. "You know how much I've been wanting to go there since it opened in June."

I had been hoping that we'd get to go there on a field trip with Camp Shemesh this past summer, but it was so overbooked that they weren't able to get us in. Instead, they took us to Kiddie Land, which had a total of three pathetic slides that you had to scoot down by pushing off the sides. Even the little slide at the community pool is better than the ones they had there.

Linda, the camp director, said that they've already made a group reservation at Splash World for next summer, but what good does that do me? Joel and I won't even be going to Camp Shemesh next year since we'll be going to sleep-away camp with Jeremy at Camp Kingman. All the disappointment and frustration I felt over the summer when I realized that I couldn't go to Splash World was now bubbling up to the surface. I had to remind myself that I just got good news and that I *was* going to be able to go there after all.

"Anyway, that's why I'm so out of it. I still can't believe it. I can't stop thinking about finally going to Splash World!"

Joel's face softened a little. We do bicker a lot, but we're also really good friends. We understand each other in a way that I guess only twins can. "Well, you'd better stop thinking about it and get that bulb to light up already. Mrs.

Morris will be around in a minute to check your work. Do you want me to help you, YaYa?" he offered.

"No, I can do it. Thanks, anyway." I softened, too. At first, I was annoyed that he had knocked me out of my daydream, but how could I stay mad at him? He was just trying to help. I untwisted my "slides" and hooked up the circuit. I had to agree with Joel. This science unit was actually a lot of fun. Much better than last year when we were just reading about weather from a textbook.

Once I got my bulb to light, Joel asked, "So when are you guys going?"

"Next Monday after school," I answered, not looking up while I admired my handiwork and gazed at the tiny glowing light.

"Next Monday? Do you mean this coming Monday or in a week and a half?" he asked. I counted the days out in my head.

"Twelve days. A week from this Monday. Why?" I finally looked up at him. Did he know something I didn't?

"You can't go then. It's Rosh Hashanah."

"No it's not; that's the following week," I answered confidently, thrilled to know something that he didn't for a change.

"Guess again," Joel said. "Rosh Hashanah begins on that Sunday night. I'm positive. I already have the TV programmed to record a special about hurricanes on the

Discovery Channel on Monday afternoon. I didn't want to miss that one."

No way! I thought to myself. I was sure he was wrong, but then again, when it comes to schedules, Joel is usually as reliable as the sun rising and setting. And in particular, when it comes to him not missing one of his shows on the Discovery Channel, he's always right.

Oh man, this was not good. I had to figure something out because there was no way I was going to miss this trip to Splash World. The question was, how could I pull it off?

4

Three Pen Tabs and a Shoebox

Mrs. Morris was back up at the front of the room, now explaining how a series circuit works. She passed around more bulbs and wires for us to connect. Joel and I each created our own series circuits easily. While we waited for Mrs. Morris to check our work, Joel went up to the front table and took an extra wire from the pile that was sitting there. He then disconnected his circuit, took a paper clip out of his backpack, and wrapped the copper end of his wire around it. He started demonstrating to me how a switch works by touching the paper clip to the other open wire and then removing it, making the light go on and off.

"What's the big deal? Why don't you just explain to Megan that it's Rosh Hashanah? I'm sure she'd understand. You can just pick another date to go to Splash World with her," Joel suggested while making the light dance on and off with his paper clip switch. He understood as well as I did that going with Megan was the only way I was going to get there, since there was no way Mom and Dad were going to take me.

"I can't do that. The whole reason they're going then is because they're taking Megan's cousins who are coming in from New York City," I told him. Then I brightened a bit, "Maybe Mom and Dad will let me go anyway. I mean, Rosh Hashanah does last for two days and all. I bet that's why they made it a two-day holiday, so that you go when it's convenient for you." I looked up hopefully at Joel.

He just looked at me with his eyebrows raised as if to say, "Are you kidding me?" He made his light flicker on and off again like he was sending a message in Morse code.

I continued. "No, seriously, I bet it's just like Passover. Like how we have two *seders*: a dinner with each side of the family. It's all about convenience and family harmony.

"That's *not* why we have two seders," he said, now giving me his "where-do-you-come-up-with-this-stuff?" look.

I ignored him. I was on a roll, and I was going to make this argument work, no matter what. I started rambling.

"Maybe there's a good reason why we have two days. Maybe Rosh Hashanah should be fun." I definitely liked how this was sounding. I got up and walked around to the front of the table to face Joel. I felt like a lawyer on one of those TV shows, making my case to the jury. I waved a pencil in Joel's face to make my point.

"Shouldn't we be celebrating the brand new year that's starting? Think about it. On December thirty-first we go to New Year's Eve parties to welcome the new year. I get that we're supposed to go to synagogue and be serious. So maybe we can do all that praying stuff on one day and then have fun on the other day for the Jewish New Year. Or maybe we should really only have to go to synagogue for one day if we've had a decent year. Maybe the second day was made up for the people who need to put in some extra prayers in case they had a really bad year. They're the ones who need a second day so they can get three pen tabs and a shoebox."

I walked back around to my spot, feeling victorious, like I just proved my argument to the justices on the Supreme Court.

Joel, however, looked at me as if I had just recited the Pledge of Allegiance in Chinese.

"Huh?"

"What do you mean, 'huh?'"

"What are you talking about? What's this 'three pen tabs and a shoebox?'" he asked, flashing me another one of his raised eyebrow stares.

"You know, what Rabbi Green was talking about the other day in Hebrew school," I reminded him. "Three pen tabs? A shoebox? How can you not remember that? He kept repeating it over and over in class."

Joel's forehead bunched up in concentration. Then, suddenly, he burst out laughing. He tried to stifle it by covering his mouth with his hand, but it was like trying to cover a garden hose with the water coming out at full power. That just made it worse and he actually laughed right out loud in class. His laughter sprayed out all over the place. He started to get hysterical and could not stop laughing. He bent over, holding his stomach, looking like he wasn't breathing. Then he snorted, which made him completely lose control. His face turned red and tears started flowing down his cheeks.

Mrs. Morris looked up from Maddie Marshall's table where she was showing her how to connect her circuit and asked, "Ellie and Joel, is everything all right with the two of you over there?"

"Yes, we're fine." I flashed her an angelic smile while subtly poking Joel with my elbow. "YoYo, cut it out," I whispered out of the side of my mouth. This only made him laugh harder.

"Need . . . to get a drink . . . water. May I . . . be excused . . . please?" Joel sputtered.

"Yes, Joel. And when you come back I expect you to have appropriate behavior in the classroom." Mrs. Morris looked over her glasses at him with a concerned and quizzical look. Joel never had bad behavior in school. He's never even seen the inside of the principal's office or been the subject of a negative phone call from a teacher to Mom and Dad.

That's not the case with me. I'm certainly not a "bad" kid, and I don't get in trouble very often, but I've gotten the "we expect better from her" or the "I'm disappointed" reports from teachers.

It's really bad when we get those teacher phone calls around dinnertime. When my dad comes home from work, he usually tries to avoid the phone. No one really calls Dad to just chit-chat. Sometimes we get calls from organizations asking for money. Most of the time when we answer the phone, it's a friend calling for Mom or one of us kids. Every now and then, however, it's one of my teachers on the other end of the line. When that happens, Dad doesn't get mad but he gets this weird look on his face where his eyebrows bunch up, the same way that Joel's do, and his eyes get a little squinty. I know it means that he's frustrated with me. We usually get those calls on days when I forgot my homework or lost a book or didn't do so well on a test I forgot to study for. I wondered if my brother was going to be the subject of a squinty-eyed phone call tonight.

Joel came back into the room with his hands in his pockets, looking down at the floor. He wouldn't look at me. Mrs. Morris finally came around to our tables to check on our circuits.

"Very nice work, you two. Your circuits look great."
Then she turned and looked directly at Joel, "Now, please,
no more outbursts out of you, Mr. Silver." She leaned in
closer to him and pulled her glasses off her nose, letting
them dangle from the chain around her neck. In almost
a whisper she said, "This is very unlike you, Joel. Are you
sure everything is all right?"

All of a sudden, Joel looked like he might burst out in
tears. He wasn't used to getting anything other than praise
and rave reviews from his teachers. Every teacher in the
school loved him and he lived for that. I don't remember
him ever being scolded at school.

"I'm fine," he mumbled, staring down at his battery as
if it was the most fascinating thing he'd ever seen in his
life. "Sorry about that, Mrs. Morris. I just thought of something funny, but I'm okay now. It won't happen again." He
glared at me, still avoiding eye contact with Mrs. Morris.
What did I do?

"I'm very glad to hear that. And thank you, Ellie, for
not disrupting the class along with your brother. I'm glad
to see that you were able to continue with your work despite Joel's antics." Mrs. Morris smiled at me. Joel glared
even harder. I could almost feel heat coming out of his
eyes. Why was he so mad at me? I didn't even know what
he had been laughing about.

Just then, the bell rang and it was time to go to our
lockers to pack up. When we got to the hall, I said to Joel,

"Hey, what just happened? Why did you crack up like that?"

"That whole 'three pen tabs and a shoebox' thing," he said with clenched teeth, looking down at his shoes as he walked. Then a small grin crept onto his face as he looked up at me. Then it grew to a full smile. "That was hilarious! I wish I could have come up with that one."

"Why was that so funny? Wasn't that what Rabbi Green was talking about?"

Joel stopped walking and turned to face me directly. "You weren't making a joke?" he asked. I shook my head. "Whoa. You really need to stop gabbing and passing notes to your friends and start paying attention in class, YaYa," he said.

"But the only time I ever get to see Abby, Mia, and Jenna is three times a week at Hebrew school. We need to talk about stuff," I defended myself.

"Well, you were so busy with your friends that you didn't hear what Rabbi Green said. He was talking about the words 'repentance and *t'shuvah*,' not three pen tabs and a shoebox. What the heck are pen tabs, anyway? And to think I was getting worried that you were taking over my job as family comedian."

"Well, um, of course I was making a joke," I said into my locker, trying to hide my embarrassment. To tell the truth, I had no idea what he was talking about, but I couldn't let Joel know that. "I just like to call them 'three pen tabs and a shoebox.' As you just proved in class, it's a much funnier name than . . . than . . . than what you just said," I stammered, still trying to act cool. I could tell that he saw right through me.

"Sure, whatever. Anyway, it's Wednesday, so you can ask Rabbi Green at Hebrew school all about the 'pen tabs' yourself. Come on, YaYa, we're going to be late."

Where have I heard that before? I closed my locker and ran down the hall after him.

5

The Longest Ride

Mom was just pulling up when we got to the curb. Jeremy was sitting in the front seat, completely absorbed in a book, and didn't even notice that we got into the car.

"Hi, Mom. Hi, Jay," I said as sweetly as I possibly could while climbing into the back seat.

"Hi, guys. How was school today?" she asked as she handed us each a juice box and a granola bar. We don't have much time between regular school and Hebrew school, so Mom always brings us a snack to eat on the way. I was glad that it was Mom driving instead of Dad. When he drives, he never remembers to bring us a snack, and I was really hungry.

"Awesome!" Joel replied as he peeled the wrapper off his granola bar. I noticed that his mood had picked up considerably since we left science class. "We played kickball at recess and I totally rocked. I got two homeruns! I kicked the ball right over Jimmy Barnett's head, and he's the tallest kid in the class. And he was way far back in the outfield. And in science class, we started working on electrical circuits." Joel started blabbering on and on about our electricity unit and how he wanted to build something using electricity for his science fair project this year. We drove for five blocks and he just kept going on about it, while I sat there trying to figure out how I was going to work Splash World into the conversation.

We passed the gas station, the supermarket, the pet store, and the mall, and he was still going. We even passed two different billboards with huge advertisements for Splash World. I had to talk to Mom!

" . . . And I got two great books from the library today. One was a joke book I've never seen before and one was about ancient Egypt. Hey, you want to hear a joke?"

Oh my gosh, he wouldn't shut up! How could I ask my question when he wouldn't stop talking? He reminded me of those auctioneer guys who talk really fast and get people to bid on stuff: *I've got one library book, one library book. Do I hear two? Two library books. Do I hear three? Going once, going twice. Sold to the young man with the juice box!*

I looked out the window and saw another gas station, three restaurants, and a hardware store zoom by. Was he ever going to take a break?

I knew I had to be smart about bringing up the topic because, of course, Mom's first reaction would be that I couldn't go to a water park when I had to be in synagogue on Rosh Hashanah. Luckily, I've been practicing Dad's skill of persuading people; I've been watching and learning from the master himself for the past ten years and eleven months. I was hoping that I'd be able to turn her "no" into a "yes," just like Dad is able to do.

The good news was that even with all his jabbering, Joel didn't mention his laugh-attack in science class or getting into trouble with Mrs. Morris. I guess he was trying to stay clear of that subject. That was fine with me because it might have put Mom in a bad mood and then I could never bring up the subject of water parks.

Joel finally stopped talking long enough to take a sip of juice. I don't think he had taken a breath since he got in the car. Suddenly it was quiet. Jeremy turned around from the front seat to look at Joel. I wondered if Jeremy wanted to see if Joel had passed out or something since he went from his non-stop chatter to complete silence.

"Done yet?" Jeremy asked in his oh-so-charming sarcastic tone. "'Cause some of us are trying to read. Oh, and FYI, no one cares about your dumb science project or your baby game of kickball."

"Jeremy, that was completely uncalled for. Don't be rude to your brother. He's just excited about his day at school," Mom defended Joel. "Besides, I remember that not too long ago you were in fifth grade and you came home just as excited about a kickball game or a science class as Joel is. Now please apologize to your brother."

"Sorry," Jeremy said with about as much sincerity in his voice as a kid thanking his teacher for extra homework.

Joel shrugged his shoulders and continued quietly sipping his juice. Jeremy returned to his book and to ignoring us. As Joel sat there silently, I had a feeling that it wasn't because Jeremy yelled at him to be quiet. I was pretty sure he was sitting there plotting how to get revenge on him. I had a hunch that the fake vomit was going to make an appearance again. I also noticed the coupon to get three dollars off your next admission to Splash World on the back of his juice box. Seriously, it was as if the ghost of Splash World was following me around.

"How about you, YaYa?" Mom asked, taking advantage of the brief moment of quiet and smiling at me through the rearview mirror. I smiled back with a big toothy grin, like a waiter who wanted an extra big tip.

"I had a good time at school today, too." *Don't mention that you left your flute on the bus and had to miss band*, I reminded myself. "I loved getting that little bulb to light up in science class. It was fun." *Okay, here goes . . .* "Speaking of fun, Mom, you'll never guess who's coming to town next weekend."

"That boy you listen to on the radio all the time? What's his name, Corey O'Connell?" Mom guessed. Jeremy snorted into his book.

"His name is Corey McDonald, Mom. You know, like the restaurant. And no, it's not him. It's even better," I replied.

Joel snickered. I swatted at his arm. My brothers make fun of me because I love listening to Corey McDonald all the time. But Corey McDonald is the best singer ever. He is so cute and has such an awesome voice. I have every single album he's ever made—all three of them.

"Someone's coming to town who's even better than Corey McNuggets?" Joel teased.

Ugh! He can be such a pain sometimes. I chose to ignore him since I was trying to get on Mom's good side. I couldn't let him get me off track. "Do you remember Megan's cousins Lindsay and Michael from New York City?"

"Sure, they were here for a couple of weeks this summer, weren't they?" Mom asked.

"Yeah, that's them."

"Wow, Lindsay and Michael rate higher than Corey McDonald? I didn't realize that you liked them so much. That's so nice that you're excited about them coming," she said.

"Well, I do like them and all," I said, "but what I'm really excited about is that Megan's parents are taking all of them to Splash World and they've invited me to come along. Isn't that great?"

"That's terrific, YaYa! I know you wanted to go all summer. How wonderful for you!" Mom said as she pulled into the synagogue parking lot. Then she got that same look on her face that she gets when she's calculating how much of a tip to leave that toothy-grinned waiter. She stopped the car and turned to look at me. "When did you say they're going?"

Uh oh, I thought to myself. *Remember, keep it cool, YaYa, keep it cool. Deep breath . . .* Then I panicked and rushed out of the car. "Um, a week from Monday, after school. Okay, got to get to class. Can't be late. Thanks for the ride, Mom," I said, and I slammed the door shut. My luck, I squeezed the juice box that was in my hand and apple juice squirted all over my jacket.

Real cool, YaYa, real cool.

6

Silly Rabbi

"N ice move, Ellie," Jeremy said, pointing at the apple juice dripping from my hand. "What was that all about?"

"Did you really not hear any of our conversation in the car?" I asked, shaking off the liquid.

"In case you didn't notice, I was reading," he said, holding up his copy of *Lord of the Rings*. "So what's the deal, you can't go see your boyfriend, Corey Mc-I-Can't-Sing-to-Save-My-Life?"

"Forget it," I told him, "you wouldn't understand." I ignored his obnoxious "boyfriend" remark. Why did he have to be so nasty all the time? To be honest, I did want to tell him about my problem because, out of all the people in our family, Jeremy would actually be the only one who would get it. When it came to amusement parks and other fun adventures, we were the only members of the Silver family who were on the same wavelength.

At least I think he would still get it. Sometimes I feel like I don't even know him anymore. Until recently, I was able to talk to him about almost anything. But I knew that those days were gone and I only had a couple of seconds left before he'd act like he didn't even know me. Once we stepped inside the building, you'd never even suspect that Jeremy was related to me and Joel, never mind that we lived in the same house. I didn't want to get into it with him when I knew he'd just walk away mid-sentence.

"Whatever," he said, shrugging his shoulders and heading toward the building.

"Bye, Jay," I said as he opened the synagogue door. Just as I expected, he waved without even looking back at us, and then entered the building. I saw him go right up to this girl named Ilana, who I know he has a crush on, even though he won't admit it. From that point on, until we got home, we would be like strangers to him, just any old invisible fifth-graders who blended in with the paint on the walls.

Joel and I walked toward the classroom wing of the synagogue together. As we walked, everyone smiled and waved at Joel. "Hey, Jokin' Joel," I heard one boy call out. Joel said "Hi" right back to everyone and he called them by their names. "What's up, Josh?" "How's it going, Alex?" *Who did he think he was, the mayor?* When he was done greeting everyone in sight, Joel turned his attention to me.

"Back there at the car, was that really your best attempt at asking Mom about going to Splash World?"

"Yeah, not too slick, huh," I said as I wiped the wet apple juice spot on my jacket with an old napkin I found in my pocket.

"Uh, that was about as slick as sandpaper," Joel replied, seeming pleased with his response. He got that same smug look on his face that he always gets when he thinks he's being clever. It drives me crazy. The good thing is that he usually snaps out of it quickly. He doesn't gloat about things for too long. He sort of gives himself an invisible pat on the back and moves on, which is exactly what he did.

"Are you going to ask Rabbi Green about why we celebrate Rosh Hashanah for two days?" he asked. "I have to admit, I'm kind of curious about that myself. I actually do know some kids who only go to services one day. Maybe it has something to do with which *shul*, which synagogue, you go to or something."

"Yeah, I'm really curious, too. It would be so great if it turns out that we don't need to do the whole Rosh Hashanah thing for both days," I said. "I know that Sophie and Marissa Klein don't go to services for two days, and they go to Temple Beth Shalom. So you may be right about different shuls having different rules."

Joel liked the rhyme that I made up accidentally. He did a little rap with it. "Maybe some shuls have different rules . . . Maybe some shuls have different rules . . . " Then he made some weird mouth noises that I think were supposed to be his attempt at making a beat. Each time he went *a-bum-bum-ch, a-bum-bum-ch*, spit came flying out of his mouth at me. Yuck! I wiped my eye with the same napkin that I used to clean up the apple juice.

When he was done rapping (and spitting) I added, "I'm also going to find out about that shoebox thing."

"T'shuvah!" Joel threw his hands up in the air, looking completely fed up with me. "How do you not know that word? We've been learning about this stuff since preschool!"

"I don't know. I mean, I know all about Rosh Hashanah, but I don't recognize that word." I admitted, kind of embarrassed. I don't seem to have the talent to learn foreign languages like my twin brother. Hebrew often confuses me. "Tell me what it is before we get to class so I don't make a total fool of myself."

"Okay," he began, "you know how we're supposed to do a lot of thinking on Rosh Hashanah? We think about how we did all year. Things we messed up on, things we want to do better from now on. And how we're supposed to say we're sorry to people that we may have hurt over the past year?"

I nodded. Of course I knew that. Like Joel said, we've been learning about saying we're sorry to our friends and family on Rosh Hashanah since we were little kids.

And even though Joel was insisting that it's not what Rabbi Green was talking about, I still had the idea of shoeboxes in my head. I mean, even if it's not part of the holiday, maybe it should be. After all, on Rosh Hashanah we do a ceremony where we throw bread into the river to symbolically "throw our sins away."

And my Grandpa Jack once told me that some people even take a live chicken and swing it over their heads in a big circle. He said that the reason they do that is because it's supposed to be as if their sins leave them and go right to the chicken instead. Then, in order to transform a bad thing into a good one, they donate the chicken to a poor family to eat. That way they actually turn it around to be a *mitzvah*, technically a "commandment" from God, but also commonly thought of as a good deed.

So I started thinking, maybe we should write down our sins, seal them in a shoebox and bury it somewhere. Hey, we Jews have lots of unusual customs. That's not any more out of the ordinary than swinging a chicken over your head!

Joel continued. "Well, when you say you're sorry and try to change your behavior, that's t'shuvah. And as for your 'three pen tabs,' the word is 'repentance.'" He said "re-pen-tance" extra slowly, as if I had just landed here from another planet and didn't speak English. *Did he really think I was that dumb?*

"Repentance is just the English word for t'shuvah," he concluded.

"So you're telling me this has nothing to do with shoeboxes?" I said. At this point, it was pretty clear to me that shoeboxes had nothing to do with it, but I was having fun annoying him. I wanted to get him back for being so full of himself before. So I went on, "Because I do usually get new shoes for the High Holidays, and they always come in boxes and I—"

"There are no shoeboxes!" Joel yelled at me in total frustration, his face turning almost pizza-sauce red.

"Okay, okay. Sorry, Little Bro," I said teasingly, throwing in one last "Little Bro" for the fun of it. "But seriously, t'shuvah is just saying you're sorry? So do you mean that just now, when I said, 'Sorry, Little Bro,' I just did this t'shuvah thingy?"

"Don't you ever listen in class? Rabbi Green said that we're supposed to think really hard about how we've disappointed ourselves, our friends, our family, and even God. Then, when we think we've figured out what we've done wrong, we ask for forgiveness and try to do things differently. So it's more than just apologizing. It's also trying to improve ourselves."

He stopped at the water fountain and took a drink. Then he continued as we walked toward our classroom, still smiling and waving at everyone along the way.

"T'shuvah really means turning around. So I guess we have to really turn ourselves around and change directions, you know, change what we're doing wrong," Joel explained.

How come he has an answer for everything? I wondered. Sometimes I wish I could know all the stuff that he does. *At least I have better hair than him*, I reminded myself. *And I'm older. And taller. Ha!* I thought, and gave myself my own invisible pat on the back. Then I refocused on our conversation.

"Okay, okay, I get it. But I'm saving my shoeboxes just in case," I said. The redness reappeared in Joel's face, making his freckles almost completely disappear. Then, just as he opened his mouth to say something back, I winked at him. All right, I didn't actually wink, but I tried. "Gotcha!" I laughed.

We got to Rabbi Green's classroom and found our seats. My friends Jenna, Mia and Abby came in and sat down next to me. Right away, we started gabbing about our favorite subject, Corey McDonald. We all love him.

"Did you hear?" Mia asked, "Corey's coming out with a new album in December!"

"Right in time for the holiday shopping season," Abby said. "I know what I want for Chanukah this year!"

"Oh my gosh, that is so awesome," Jenna said. "I can't wait to hear it!"

"So you guys," I chimed in, "I hate to change the subject from Corey, because believe me, I could talk about him all day, but I have to tell you about my latest dilemma before class starts." Just as I began telling them about Splash World, out of the corner of my eye, I saw Rabbi Green come into the classroom holding something behind his back. I kept talking because I figured I had a minute or two before class started. Some kids didn't even notice that he had walked into the room at all, but that didn't last for long.

Rabbi Green, like always, pulled his big wooden chair out from under his desk. But what surprised us was when he stepped on the chair and then climbed up and stood right on top of his desk!

"What the heck?" Jenna mouthed to me.

I shrugged back. I was just as bewildered.

Rabbi Green was so tall that his black curly hair almost touched the ceiling. He called out in a loud voice, "*T'kiah!*" Then he blew a long loud note with the *shofar*, a ram's horn, which was what he had been hiding when he entered the room. Next he called out, "*Sh'varim!*" and blew three shorter blasts. Then he called, "*T'ruah!*" and he made nine short, quick toots, which sounded like "toot-toot-toot-toot-toot-toot-toot-toot-toot." Finally he called, "*T'kiah g'dolah!*" and held a note for a long time. I started counting and if I had to guess, I'd say he went for about twenty seconds. Talk about an entrance! I couldn't believe he stood on top of the desk. I'd never seen a teacher do anything like that before.

By now, he certainly had everyone's attention. Some kids started giggling. I heard my friend Dahlia, who was sitting behind me, whisper something about Rabbi Green losing it.

I sure hope he's not losing it, I thought to myself. This is the man I'm counting on for some answers. This is the man who is going to help me explain to my parents why it's totally fine for me to go and have fun on Rosh Hashanah. Rabbi Green is my ticket to Splash World. I know he'll be able to help me out. That is, if he hasn't completely gone off his rocker.

7

Soul Patrol

Good afternoon, *yeladim*," Rabbi Green said in his jolly, booming voice. He always calls us yeladim. It means "children" in Hebrew. Rabbi Green likes to use as many Hebrew words as he can when he's speaking to us. I have to admit that I have learned a lot of new vocabulary that way.

Rabbi Green also likes to call us by our Hebrew names. That's probably the only time anyone ever calls us Yael and Yoel outside of our house. When we first started Hebrew school two years ago, some kids caught on to our matching names and we did get teased about it a little. Luckily no one makes a big deal about it anymore. And for sure, no one knows that at home we're called YaYa and YoYo. I think I would just die if that got out.

Some kids were still giggling and others were just staring at Rabbi Green as he climbed down from the desk and hopped to his feet. They were probably wondering the same thing that I was: What kind of a teacher stands on top of a desk like that? What's the deal?

Sometimes when people think of a rabbi, they think of an old man with a long white beard. That's not Rabbi Green. (It's also not Rabbi Levine at Sophie and Marissa's shul. She'd look pretty funny with a beard!) I think Rabbi Green is a little younger than my dad. He wears a *kippah* that sort of gets lost in his dark bushy hair, but he wears a different one every day, and I always look forward to seeing which one he'll have on.

He has one that looks like a soccer ball and one with a smiley face on it. Some of them have cartoon characters or superheroes. You never know what you'll find up there. I craned my neck to see which one he was wearing. When he bent over to straighten out his pants, I saw that it had a picture of a robot on it. The funny thing about that one was that the robot was wearing a kippah!

Rabbi Green always has a warm smile on his face and he never seems to be in a bad mood. I always feel like he's glad to see me. He's pretty cool for a grown-up, and especially for a rabbi. He has two young daughters and we often see him playing with them at the park. I've also seen him riding his bike around the neighborhood and playing soccer at the field behind our school. His first name is Jonathan, but he goes by Yoni. Some kids like to call him Rabbi Yoni and he seems to be fine with that, but Joel and I are more comfortable calling him Rabbi Green.

"So did I get your attention?" Rabbi Green asked. He was trying to catch his breath after that long t'kiah g'dolah. His face was a little bit pink from all that blowing.

Everyone nodded. *Maybe he fell off his bicycle without a helmet on*, I thought to myself.

"Good." he said. "That's the whole point of the shofar. The shofar is supposed to be like an alarm clock. It's there to wake us up from the comfort of our daily lives and shake things up a bit. Anybody know when we blow this thingamabob?"

"On Rosh Hashanah," called out Know-It-All Hannah.

"Duh!" Micah Salzman muttered under his breath.

"Yes, Chana, that's true. But did you know that we also blow it each morning during our daily morning services? Right now, at this time in the Jewish calendar, we are in the Hebrew month of *Elul*, the last month of the year. The shofar 'goes off' like an alarm clock all month long so that we wake up with a start and get ready for a new day, or in this case, a new year."

"Is there a snooze button on that thing?" Ethan Meyerson joked. The whole class laughed.

"Well, I wouldn't say that there's a snooze button, Eitan," Rabbi Green chuckled, "but I suppose you could say that it is almost as if we've fallen into a peaceful snooze-state since last Rosh Hashanah and Yom Kippur. The shofar is supposed to make us wake up and take notice of what we've been doing, and to start thinking about how we'd like to improve the way we do things. It's a chance for us to take stock of ourselves. We can continue with the things we're pleased with and we can change the things that aren't going so well."

Aha, I thought, *so he isn't losing it after all.* Meanwhile, Joel looked over at me from across the room. He raised his eyebrows and pointed his chin in Rabbi Green's direction as if to say, "See, that's what I was talking about."

"It sounds like a lot of work. Who has the time to sit around and think about stuff like that? And how are we supposed to remember what we've done all year?" asked Abby.

"Actually," Rabbi Green responded, "I'd say it's a wonderful gift. It's something that's built into our calendar that forces us to stop what we're doing and make the time to do some thinking. Time that we wouldn't necessarily take otherwise. And you're right, it may be hard to remember *everything,* and it *is* a lot of work. But it's important work that needs to be done."

He paused for a moment, looked around at everyone in the room and then said, "Just think, in your house someone has to clean the toilets, right?"

Everyone groaned and some kids made sick faces. Ari Wolff, one of Joel's best friends, put his finger in his mouth like he was gagging.

"Well, imagine if nobody did that job. The bathroom would be a nasty, smelly mess. It may not be fun, easy or even pleasant, but we're sure glad when it's done, aren't we?"

Heads bobbed up and down in agreement.

"Yeah, but I don't want to be the one who has to do that job," said Matthew Steinberg, who was sitting next to Joel. Lots of kids snickered. Ari gave Matthew a high five.

"And I bet that your mother, your father, the house-keeper or whoever it is that scrubs your toilet has other things that they'd much rather be doing as well. But it needs to get done. And let's be honest, cleaning out our souls is a lot less messy than cleaning the toilet," Rabbi Green said.

"What do you mean by 'cleaning out our souls'?" Mia asked.

"Does anyone remember our discussion about t'shuvah from last week?" Rabbi Green asked the class. Once again, Joel looked over at me again with his smug "See, what-did-I-tell-you?" look. I wrinkled my nose at him. Joel raised his hand.

"Yes, Yoel," Rabbi Green said, calling on him.

"T'shuvah is when we turn ourselves around. It's when we decide to change the way we're doing things and try to do them better. It's kind of like when our parents make us clean out our closets. Now and then, we find cool things we forgot we had and we might even find things we wish we didn't. Sometimes the things we find can turn out to be rather disgusting." Joel looked sideways at me with a sneaky grin.

I knew just what he was getting at. He was talking about the hard, half-eaten peanut butter sandwich I found in the back of my closet last month. Or maybe it was the unrecognizable apple—at least I'm pretty sure it was an apple—that I found in a Ziploc bag that must have fallen out of the pocket of my backpack and stayed in my closet until I found it. It was more like mushy, brownish-gray applesauce by then. All I can say was that in both cases it was gross. I mean really, really gross! At least they were all sealed up and didn't smell bad. Not like Jeremy's skateboard beanie hat.

I narrowed my eyes and gave him a look as if to say, "Don't you dare share that with the class." Thankfully he didn't. I had a feeling that if it weren't for this whole discussion about changing our behavior he would have totally embarrassed me. I think he was working on his own t'shuvah already. Thank goodness!

"Very good, Yoel. I like the image of cleaning out the closet," Rabbi Green said. Joel beamed. "And I'm not sure I want to know what you found in your closet either." Rabbi Green wagged his finger at Joel with a chuckle.

I saw Joel's knuckles turn white as he gripped the sides of his desk. His face turned so red that there was no trace of his freckles. I knew that he was just dying to stand up, point at me and tell everyone that it wasn't his closet, it was mine. But he just sat there and smiled back at Rabbi Green, red face and all. *Boy, do I owe him one*, I thought.

The discussion about t'shuvah went on for a while longer. I was glad when we were finally done talking about cleaning toilets and closets. I was also really glad that Joel had caught me up to speed about the word "t'shuvah" so that I didn't embarrass myself and ask about the shoeboxes. I don't know how I missed that whole discussion last time, but I was sure grateful that Joel helped me out there.

Finally, Rabbi Green asked if anyone had any other questions about Rosh Hashanah. I shot my hand up as fast as I could.

"I do," I said.

The moment had arrived. I could finally get the answers I needed so that I could make my case and get to Splash World. Suddenly I felt nervous. I could practically feel that tingly feeling in my stomach, just as if I was zooming my way down Dead Man's Drop. I'm never nervous in class or too shy to ask a question. But this one was different. It was a matter of life or death! All right, it wasn't really, but I was so nervous about it, it almost felt like it was. I took a deep breath.

Okay, here goes.

8

Shofar, So Good

"What's your question, Yael?" Rabbi Green asked.

I was so anxious I could hardly stand it. My legs seemed to have a mind of their own by the way they were shaking under my desk, and I couldn't stop jiggling the pencil in my hand. "Rabbi Green, why do we have two days of Rosh Hashanah? I mean, do we *really* need to go to shul for two days?" I finally asked.

"That's a very good question," he began. "Well, as you know, the Jewish calendar is based on a lunar cycle, which means that it's based on the phases of the moon. Back in the days of the Temple in Jerusalem, people didn't know exactly when the old moon or month was ending and the new one was beginning. The group of rabbis who set the religious laws, known as the Sanhedrin, was responsible for announcing when it was a new moon. Then they had to get the message out to all the people who lived in other communities outside of Jerusalem."

"No cell phones or email, huh?" Ethan joked.

"That sure would have made things easier, wouldn't it?" Rabbi Green said. "In order to be absolutely, one hundred percent sure that everyone was celebrating on the correct day, it was decided that two days would be observed. This way, no matter what, they would get it right."

"Seriously?" I asked, starting to get my hopes up. "So are you saying that nowadays we could just do one day since we have computers and stuff? Can't we just figure out exactly which is the right day? It sounds to me like we really only need one day after all." I could feel my heart beating a little faster. *So far, so good.*

"Interestingly, that is how some people see it. In many Reform congregations, they do observe only one day." Now it was my turn to give Joel a knowing look. That's why Sophie and Marissa Klein only go for one day.

Rabbi Green explained further, "People who aren't Jewish might think that all Jewish people practice Judaism alike. But actually, there are lots of different groups of Jews and each one does things a little differently. In the United States the three biggest branches of Judaism are called Conservative, Reform and Orthodox. Even right here in our neighborhood, we have one of each type of congregation. As you know, we here at Ohav Zedek are Conservative. Temple Beth Shalom is Reform and Ahavas Yisroel is Orthodox."

Right then I chuckled to myself very quietly, not like Joel's outburst earlier, because I remembered how confused I was when I was little. I have cousins who are Orthodox who used to live near us before they moved to Israel. At the same time, my parents were good friends with Dr. Markus, who is now Jeremy's orthodontist. When I was really little, I used to think that my cousins went to an "Orthodontist" shul. Turns out that Dr. Markus goes to a Conservative synagogue and my Orthodox cousins don't know a thing about dentistry. Go figure!

"And while they only observe one day at some Reform synagogues like Temple Beth Shalom," Rabbi Green continued, "most Conservative and Orthodox congregations and some Reform congregations have maintained the custom of observing for two days. Even in Israel, where they celebrate all other holidays for only one day when we celebrate for two, they also observe Rosh Hashanah for two days. In fact, some people don't even count it as two days. Some say the two days of Rosh Hashanah are actually considered to be one very long day."

Rabbi Green kept on talking, but I didn't hear any more of his explanation. All I heard was the background noise of his voice droning on. As he talked, I imagined my waterslides crumbling and falling apart. I saw them slowly sinking into a pool as I stood and watched from the side. My dream was drowning.

Finally I heard him say, "Besides, it gives us an extra day to do some good quality thinking, as well as an extra day to celebrate and be with our families and the people we love. We can never get enough of that, can we?" he smiled.

I smiled back politely, but in my head I couldn't help but think, *Family, shmamily. How much time do I need to be with my family? I'd rather be going down Terror Plummet!*

9

Stories From the Silver Lining

Dad got that scrunchy look on his face again. Joel and I looked at each other across the dinner table, Joel looking a little bit pale. I quickly ran through the day's events to see if it was possible that this phone call was about me. It could have been Mr. Foss calling to rat on me about not having my flute for band practice. Joel's face got whiter and whiter as Dad's got redder and redder.

"Yes, this is Mark Silver," he said into the phone, sounding annoyed.

"Uh oh," Joel mouthed to me. Oh yeah, this one was about him and his laugh attack in Mrs. Morris's class, I figured.

"Look, I don't want to be rude, but I have to interrupt you here," he said into the phone. "We have already given a sizable donation to your organization. In fact, we support your efforts every year. I would appreciate it if you would please take me off your calling list. I much prefer to make my donations on my own schedule. Thank you." Dad put down the phone, probably a little harder than he needed to. Joel let out a relieved sigh, probably a little louder than he needed to.

"I can't stand those fundraising phone calls. I understand that they need to raise money, but they're preaching to the choir. I already gave them a donation. A fairly generous one, in fact," Dad said, returning to the table. "And why do they have to call right at dinner time?" He plopped down heavily in his chair. But then, almost magically, his whole face changed. All the worry lines that had crept up on his forehead disappeared and his anger seemed to melt away the minute the napkin touched his lap. He loves family dinnertime. For Dad, coming to the dinner table is his most peaceful and relaxing time of the day. His whole face transformed, as if he had just left the noise, crowds, and stress of a huge traffic jam behind and entered a quiet, serene garden. He took a deep breath and smiled.

"So let me tell you what happened at the store today," Dad said, back in his usual cheerful voice. Dad owns a small bookstore in our neighborhood called The Silver Lining. (Get it? *Silver* Lining—because our last name is Silver? You see, the corny names never end in my family!)

Dad's a great salesman who enjoys coming up with cute gimmicks and deals to get customers into his store. I only hope that when I grow up, I love going to work as much as my dad does. He enjoys helping each of his customers find the perfect book. Whether it's about gardening or horoscopes, a romance novel or a murder mystery, Dad likes to make recommendations for people.

"So this woman had walked into the store a couple of weeks ago, looking for a good novel set in medieval times. I recommended that one that you loved so much, Deb. Remember, *Star of the Knights?*"

"Oh yeah, I did love that one," Mom said.

"That's what I tried to tell her but she didn't believe me. She just said that she had never heard of that author and that she wasn't interested. But you know me, I couldn't just give up," Dad said with a mischievous look on his face.

"Yeah, so what did you do? Did you suggest another one?" Joel asked.

"No, I tried something new," Dad said, taking a forkful of meatloaf. "I told her to take it for free on the condition that she come back and let me know if I was right or not."

"No offense, Dad," Jeremy chimed in, "but giving books away for free won't exactly pay for me to go to camp this summer. I guess it's a good thing Mom's art business is doing so well this year."

Joel rolled his eyes and I nodded across the table to him.

"So what happened?" Mom asked, ignoring Jeremy's comment.

"She came running into the store today, almost in tears."

"She hated it that much? Was she mad at you?" Joel interrupted.

"No, she had just finished it and loved it so much that she ran over to the store to tell me. She said she was so excited that I found such a perfect book for her. And she loved this new author. She especially enjoyed the ending, which she said was so beautiful she was still crying from it. To make a long story short, I recommended a few more titles to her. Let's just say, she left the store today with two very heavy shopping bags and a promise that she'd be back with her entire book group. Oh, did I mention she insisted on hardcover copies?" he added with a smile that made him look like a kid who had just won the national spelling bee.

"Oh, Mark, that's fabulous!" Mom gushed.

"Cool. Camp Kingman, here I come," said Mr. Self-Absorbed.

"Dad, you could talk a snowman into buying a furnace," Joel joked.

"Oh, and one more thing. I found some great large-print copies of *Star of the Knights* to donate to The Davidson Residence," Dad finished. The Davidson Residence is the nursing home where my great-grandmother Pearl lived until she died. Dad spends a lot of time there bringing books that he donates. Sometimes he reads books to the people who live there.

When Dad was done with his story, Joel started babbling about how he was so great at kickball today. Since I had heard this one time too many during our car ride earlier, I pretty much tuned him out. Of course, my mind instantly zipped back to Splash World, and I realized that trying to get my parents to let me go was about as likely as a water park suddenly sprouting up out of the garden in our backyard. It just wasn't going to happen.

Even though it was all I could think of, I wasn't going to mention it again. At least not until I could come up with a good strategy. I was surprised when Mom brought it up. As she was handing me the bowl of mashed potatoes, she said, "Honey, I don't know if you realized this or not, but Megan and her family are going to Splash World during Rosh Hashanah. I hate to break it to you, but you won't be able to go then. I'm sorry, sweetie."

And that was it. There was no room for discussion, questions, arguments or even good old-fashioned begging. It was as plain and simple as knowing that a red light means stop. I couldn't go. Still, I decided to give it one last shot. I felt like I had to at least try. Maybe the light was really yellow and only just about to turn red. Maybe if I pushed a little bit I could get through to them.

It couldn't hurt to try, right?

Invasion of the Messy Snatchers

"What's this all about?" Dad asked, picking up the napkin from his lap and wiping his mouth with it.

"Megan invited me to go to Splash World with her next Monday."

"Is that the new water park that just opened near the airport?" Dad asked.

Now it was Mom's turn. "Yes, but the timing is most unfortunate. They are going during Rosh Hashanah, so obviously the answer has to be no."

"Mom, Dad," I said with my best sad-puppy-dog eyes, "is there any way that I can go? I mean, do I really need to do two whole days of Rosh Hashanah?" I made sure to sound sad and not whiny. As Mom always says, "Whining does not lead to winning."

Joel looked up from his plate and gave me a look that said, "What do you think you're doing, YaYa?" Even Jeremy looked at me. It was clear that he was also interested in our discussion. Lately, it seemed, if it wasn't about skate-boarding, video games, or girls, he didn't participate much in our family conversations. And usually our family conversations were not about skateboarding, video games, or girls. Yet he was clearly interested. He didn't stop eating, of course, being the twelve-and-a-half-year-old eating machine that he is, but he was definitely listening to every word.

I kept going despite Joel's look. I couldn't stop now. "Of course, I'll go to services. I know that Rosh Hashanah is important. I could even go Monday morning because they're not going until the afternoon." Then I threw in one last plea, "Would you at least think about it?" I glanced over to see Jeremy picking a big piece of broccoli out of his braces. Gross! If I wasn't already about to cry, that might have done the trick on its own.

Dad put his hand on top of mine. "I'm sorry, honey, but this one is out of the question. It's non-negotiable. And you know that I like making deals as much as the next guy," he said. "But aside from the fact that Rosh Hashanah is one of our most important and holy holidays, it's a special time for us as a family, and you need to be with us. We can't have our holiday without you."

"But I've been waiting for an opportunity like this for months!" Time to start using my Dad-skills and throw in a sales pitch. It's all in the marketing, as Dad always says. "The best part is that I can go to the water park and you don't even have to take me! And I'll use my allowance money to get in, so it won't cost you a dime. It's a great deal for you! It's a win-win situation!"

"That does sound good, YaYa, but, our answer is still no," Dad said.

"But what about—" I started to protest.

"Sorry, sweetie," Dad cut me off. "It's not going to work. Not on Rosh Hashanah. You know that."

"Not even if—" I tried again.

"Sorry." He picked up my hand and kissed it. So much for my masterful sales pitch. Time to try the divide and conquer method. If maybe I could get one of them on my side, I'd have a chance.

"Mom," I said pleading softly, turning to face her directly as if no one else was even in the room, "you know how important this is to me. I'm willing to do anything. I'll make dinners for a month, I'll do everyone's laundry . . . except maybe for Jeremy's," I added for comic relief. She chuckled. "Please, think about it. I'll do whatever you ask me to. That's how much it means to me." I felt tears welling up in my eyes.

"YaYa, I know you feel that this trip to Splash World is important to you. But Rosh Hashanah is even more important to us as a Jewish family. It's a really big deal. Even bigger than the best water park on earth." Mom passed me a tissue.

"I hate to have to say no to you," she continued, "especially after your very tempting laundry offer. And, even if you *did* agree to do Jay's laundry as well, I still have to agree with Dad. You should probably call Megan after dinner. Make sure you thank her and her parents because it was so nice of them to invite you. Maybe you can try again another time."

Yeah, whatever, I thought sadly as I wiped my eyes. But what I said in almost a whisper was, "Okay, Mom, I will."

I ate a few bites of my meatloaf and mashed potatoes, which is usually one of my favorite meals, but I couldn't enjoy it at all. I broke the slice of meatloaf into tiny pieces and slid them around on my plate, trying to make it look like I had eaten more than I really did. After a while, I asked to be excused to go and call Megan.

I went to my room and flopped on the bed. And then I cried. I don't know how long I was lying there, but it felt like forever. I could hear my parents clearing the dishes from the table. I heard Jeremy's heavy footsteps coming up the stairs and down the hall to his room. His door thudded closed and music instantly blasted through the walls.

After a good, long cry, I lifted my head from my soaking wet pillow. I took a few deep breaths and rolled out of bed. Then I got busy. I managed to find every activity possible to avoid making that call.

I was secretly hoping that maybe, miraculously, my parents would look at each other and suddenly realize that

I could go. I pictured my mom and dad throwing open my door with huge smiles, bursting into my room with the news. "Guess what?" they'd say. "We just figured out that you don't really have to observe the holiday for two days. And we can have our dinner without you for one night. You can go down all those crazy water slides after all. Go and have a great time, YaYa!"

They never came in.

I found lots of things to do in my room. I did my homework—all of it, even my math. I set up my music stand and got ready to practice my flute. Then I remembered that I couldn't do that since I had left my flute on the bus. So I put the music stuff away.

I cleaned up my desk and made my bed. I fluffed up my pillow and shook it around a few times to try to dry the wet spot from my tears. I placed it neatly against the headboard and took a couple of my favorite stuffed animals that had been strewn about on the floor and propped them up in front of the pillow.

Next, I got down on the floor, reached under my bed and felt around for whatever might be under there. Luckily, I did not find any old food. I did, however, find a copy of *Starring Sally J. Freedman as Herself*, the school library book that I lost last year. I organized all of my games and put all of the game and puzzle pieces back into the boxes where they belonged. The top hat from my Monopoly game was finally reunited with the dog and the shoe. When I was done with that, I alphabetized my Corey McDonald CDs—all three of them.

Before I knew it, it was eight-thirty. I put my homework and the library book into my backpack. I slipped into the bathroom and took a shower, remembering to use conditioner so that maybe I wouldn't have another knot-battle in the morning. I got into my pajamas and returned to my room. I had successfully avoided calling Megan. I looked around my room and saw that I had also successfully made my bedroom look like it belonged in a store catalogue. It was neat. It was organized. It looked like someone else's room.

Dad knocked and called through the door, "Hey, YaYa, time to get ready for bed, kiddo." I opened the door to let him in. He just stood there, his eyes wide and his mouth open. Then he called out, "Hey, Deb, come quick! I think we've been invaded by aliens or trolls or something. Someone's been in YaYa's room. And they took her with them and replaced her with this identical but neat clone."

Mom came rushing over, wiping her hand on a dish-towel. "What's wrong? What did you say, Mark? Is every-thing—" She stopped in the doorway next to my dad and just stared. The two of them looked pretty hysterical just standing there, staring at me and my room.

Mom came over and felt my forehead. When she was finally convinced that I was not sick, and Dad accepted that I had not been abducted by aliens, we laughed. We laughed for a long, long time, and it felt really good. After crying to the point that I felt like I had no tears left, it felt so good to laugh.

Joel heard the commotion and came in to see what was going on. Dad told him about his alien theory. This, of course, reminded Joel of a joke. "What do Martians toast around the campfire?" he asked. Blank stares from all of us. "Mars-mallows! Get it? *Mars*-mallows, you know, marshmallows?" We groaned because it was such a bad joke. But then we all looked at each other and started cracking up.

We were making quite a racket. I guess Jeremy was able to hear us over his music. He peeked in. "What's up?" he said in his slow, cool voice, which was getting deeper and lower each day. Then he stopped and looked around. "Whoa, dude, what happened here?"

The night that had started out very sad and depressing ended up being a lot of fun. I remembered what I knew all along—that spending some quality time with my family, as Rabbi Green had mentioned, can be great. I cuddled up in bed and did the *Sh'ma* prayer with my dad, like we do every night. Then I rolled over and went to sleep. I still felt bad about Splash World but decided not to worry about telling Megan the bad news until the morning. Instead, I fell asleep thinking about Martians eating marshmallows.

One Freaky Morning

The next morning I had a very strange dream. A miniature Rabbi Green, about the size of a hamster, had climbed up on my nightstand and started blowing his shofar. I kept hearing that shofar tooting over and over again. Unlike when he did it in class, he wouldn't stop. I kept hearing, "Toot. Toot. Toot." It was driving me nuts.

Finally I woke up enough to realize that it was my alarm clock going off. I smacked the snooze button as I do each morning. I was groggy and not completely awake. All of a sudden, in a surge of panic, I sat straight up in my bed, my heart pounding so hard that I could practically feel it through my pajama top. I thought that I had just crushed my hamster-sized Hebrew school teacher with my hand! Well, now I was wide awake. It usually takes me about four snooze cycles before I wake up. I am *not* a morning person. I like to sleep for as long as I possibly can. But there's nothing like waking up in a state of shock to get your blood going in the morning.

There was no going back to sleep after that. I got out of bed and looked around my room. For a minute I didn't know where I was. *Whose room is this?* I thought to myself. Then, slowly, it all came back to me. I remembered cleaning up and keeping myself busy so I wouldn't have to call Megan. Of course, that reminded me that I would have to tell her the bad news later on the bus. I dragged myself to my dresser, got dressed and went downstairs for breakfast. It was only ten after seven and our bus comes forty minutes later. I usually get to the kitchen at about ten minutes before it arrives (that is, when I actually have time for breakfast). This was my all-time record.

I took out a bowl, a spoon, a box of cereal and the milk. *This isn't too bad,* I thought to myself. *Check me out, I'm sitting down and eating breakfast. Mom isn't bugging me to get out of bed. This is nice!* As I ate, I started practicing how I would tell Megan the bad news. Out loud.

"So now you're talking to yourself? You're getting weirder and weirder each day," Joel said as he walked into the kitchen. I didn't notice that he had come in because I was so caught up in my thoughts, figuring out what to say.

I was embarrassed. He really has a knack for making me feel dumb. I didn't say anything back. I just finished eating, cleared my dishes, and walked right past Joel on my way to brush my teeth. I made sure to stand extra tall as I passed him.

Mom came into the kitchen, already showered and dressed, as I was on my way out. She had a huge smile on her face. "What a great surprise this is! I love not fighting with you to get out of bed. Way to go, YaYa!" she said as she headed to the coffee maker.

"Wow, you're ready early," I noted.

"I have two back-to-back meetings with potential clients, and then I'm seeing Aunt Rachel to go over the artwork for her wedding invitations. It's going to be a crazy morning."

"Oh, I know all about crazy mornings," I said as I made my way to the bathroom.

Before I knew it, I had eaten my breakfast *and* washed up. The conditioner I used in the shower last night did the trick. My brush slid as easily through my hair as the greased watermelon slipped through my fingers in the pool during color war at camp. And speaking of watermelons, no more watermelon sized knots! I was victorious over the hairy beast! Hooray!

I was ready to walk out the door, and it was only seven thirty-five. I may not be getting weirder and weirder as Joel said, but this morning was definitely freaky. I went back to my room and made my bed, which I never have time to do. I had nothing else to do so I decided to walk to the bus stop. I called out to Joel in a rap, "YoYo, Little Bro, I'm ready to go."

"Go ahead. I'll catch up. We still have at least ten minutes," he called back. "Who *are* you, anyway? And what did you do with my sister?" Then he added, "And stop calling me Little Bro!"

I kissed Mom goodbye. She was standing at the door with her coffee cup in her hand. "Bye-bye, sweetie," she said. "This was a wonderful start to your day. I hope the rest of your day goes as well."

"Thanks, Mom," I said. But I knew that it was all downhill from here.

12

School Bus Surprises

I walked slowly to the bus stop. No one was there. I could see a shadowy figure all the way down the block walking toward me, which I figured was probably Haley Walters coming from her house at the other end of the street. I couldn't believe I was going to be the first one there. I've never gotten to the bus stop before Haley. This really was shaping up to be one strange day.

By the time Roy pulled up, both Haley and Joel were with me. They looked at their watches and then at one another, shared puzzled looks and shrugged their shoulders. Even Roy seemed to do a double take when he saw me get on the bus first.

"Good morning, Miss Ellie," he said with his usual cheerful smile. "I see you kept your promise from yesterday."

I had actually forgotten all about the promise I had made yesterday. But once he said that, I remembered that

I said I'd beat my time and get to the bus earlier. "Yep," I said, "I sure did. Right on time today."

"Not just on time, you're even early," Roy said. "You beat your old time by three whole minutes and two seconds." I had no idea if he was just making that up or if he really was keeping track of my time, but I liked playing our little game.

I started to walk to my seat when Roy said to me, "I left you a present."

There, sitting in my spot, in the third seat on the right by the window, was a Macy's shopping bag. *Roy got me a present from Macy's? How did I get so lucky to have such a nice bus driver?*

I went over to the bag and peered in. I was very excited and curious. I love presents—who doesn't? I couldn't believe it. In the bag waiting for me was something even better than anything available for sale on a rack at Macy's. There, in the bag, was my flute case. And under that was my favorite Niagara Falls hat, the one I thought I'd never see again.

"Wow! Thanks, Roy! I didn't even know that I'd lost my hat on the bus. Thanks for taking such good care of me," I said before sitting down.

Roy turned around and winked at me. "It's my pleasure to help one of my favorite customers."

I did my blinky-winky thing back to him. By now all the kids were sitting in their seats so I sat down, too, and

Roy started driving. I put my hat on, opened the flute case, looked at my flute and then closed the case. I realized that I still had about nine minutes left before Megan got on the bus and had nothing to keep me busy. Then I remembered the *Sally J. Freedman* library book that I put in my backpack. I had lost it last spring, as in when I was in fourth grade. And to be honest, I never even read it. So I took it out and started reading. And what do you know? It was actually very good.

I was really getting into the story when the bus stopped. I could see Megan from my window. She looked up and saw me and waved. I waved back, but at the same time I got that sick tickly feeling in my stomach that I had in Rabbi Green's class yesterday. I don't know why I was so nervous, but for some reason I was. I put a bookmark in to save my page. I was surprised to see that I was already almost one fourth of the way through the book. That was fast. I closed the book and put it away.

Megan got on the bus and came right over to my seat. "Hey, Ellie. What's going on? No homework?" She sounded surprised.

"Believe it or not, I got it all done last night. I even cleaned my room."

"I think I'm going to faint," she said, putting her hand on her chest and gasping as if she was in a horror movie or something. She thinks she's pretty funny.

"All right, that's enough, Drama Queen," I said. "Look, I even found the library book that I lost last year."

"Wow! What's gotten into you? I don't know that I ever remember you cleaning your room," Megan said.

"Ha ha, very funny," I said back. "You know, every five years, whether it needs it or not, my room gets cleaned." I can be a smart alec too.

"Well, that was very brave of you. So what made you take on this heroic feat?" she asked.

"Funny you should ask," I said. "I was actually keeping myself busy so that I wouldn't have to call you with my bad news."

"Bad news? Well, that's okay. I didn't have time to talk last night anyway. I was so busy working on the book report that's due tomorrow," Megan said. "I was up until almost ten o'clock working on it. I can't believe you had time to clean your room. I'm impressed."

"*We have a book report? What book report?*" I shouted just a bit too loud. Dylan Cooper and a few other kids across the aisle turned around to look at me. "Well, now it looks like I have another thing to worry about. I didn't even remember that we had one due tomorrow."

"Oh, sorry," she said. "So I guess now you have two bits of bad news. What were you going to tell me?"

I took my Niagara Falls hat off and ran my fingers over the stitched letters on the front. Anything to avoid looking Megan in the eye. "I can't go with you guys to Splash

World," I mumbled, staring at the picture of the rainbow at the bottom of the Falls.

"What'd you say? I couldn't hear you," Megan said.

I looked up at her. "I said that I can't go with you to Splash World. Next Monday is Rosh Hashanah and I have to be with my family. I'm really bummed, but there's no way that I can go with you," I said quietly.

"No way! Are you sure?" she asked really loudly. Dylan looked over at us again. "Are you sure?" she repeated, quieter this time, shooing Dylan to turn around and mind his own business.

"Yeah, I'm sure."

"You mean, like a hundred percent sure or just probably sure?"

"No, I mean, like two hundred percent sure. It would kind of be like you not being with your family on Easter. I really can't skip it."

"Oh man, I can't believe you can't go. That stinks even more than the book report. I'm sorry I didn't realize it was your holiday. What a bummer. We'll have to try to go another time."

"Believe me, I'm sorry too," I said.

"Well, at least you get to miss some school, right?" she said.

"Yeah, that's true." *Hmm, I hadn't thought about that. I do get to miss two days of school, don't I?* I thought to myself. Okay, that's something, I guess. But then again, I don't really hate school the way a lot of other kids do. I actually like going. But two days off is two days off. I can't really complain about that, can I?

"All right, enough about that," I was dying to change the subject, even to another bad one. "Tell me about the book report. Are you sure my class is doing it too?"

"Yeah, Jamie Anderson from your class and I were just talking about it the other day. We're both doing the same book. The good news is that you can do it on any book you want. Have you read anything good lately?"

I looked down at *Sally J. Freedman* in my backpack and pulled it out to show her, "Yeah, I'm in the middle of a good book right now. I can finish it up pretty quickly."

I got off the bus at school with my baseball cap on my head, my flute case in my backpack, my newly found, used-to-be-lost library book in my hand and a stomach that wasn't all tied up in knots anymore. Telling Megan the news wasn't as awful as I thought it would be.

Now I couldn't believe I had a book report to do. I started to feel that tingly feeling in my stomach all over again, just thinking about it.

I guess the library will have to wait a few more days for *Sally*, I thought as I headed up the steps to school.

13

Get Ready, Get (The Table) Set, Go!

On Sunday afternoon, one whole week before Rosh Hashanah, Mom started setting the table for the holiday. I know that seems a little ridiculous, but she does this before every big holiday. She says that it's one thing that she can get done early and check off her to-do list. She tends to get a little overwhelmed when we host a lot of company, and we were expecting more than twenty people at our house for dinner on the second night of Rosh Hashanah.

Every year Grandma Ruth and Grandpa Jack, my Dad's parents, have us over to their house for the first night of the holiday. On the second night of Rosh Hashanah we have dinner at our house and everyone comes to us, including my aunts, uncles, and cousins from my mom's side of the family, as well as other guests that my parents invite.

Aunt Julie—Mom's sister—and her family go to Temple Beth Shalom, the same synagogue that Sophie and Marissa go to, so on Rosh Hashanah we only see them when they come over for dinner. We call my mom's parents *Bubby* and *Zayde* Miller. They live in Florida. Some years they come to visit us for the High Holidays, but this year they're staying home. I really like it when we have both sets of grandparents with us, especially for the holidays. Bubby and Zayde promised to try to come for Passover and, of course, they'll be here for Jeremy's bar mitzvah.

I was sitting in the living room, reading the Sunday comics, when Mom called to me. I walked into the dining room to find her ironing wrinkles out of the tablecloth directly on the table.

"YaYa, can you please look for the silver polish in the cabinet in the hall, and bring it, and a clean rag, to the kitchen for me?" she asked.

I knew what was coming next.

"Oh, and while you're at it, would you and YoYo please go downstairs and bring up the boxes of good silverware from the basement? Thanks, sweetie."

Wait for it . . .

"And would the two of you please polish the silverware?"

Like clockwork, I tell you. Every year it's the same thing.

"I'm on it," I said as I headed up the stairs to get my brother.

I knocked on Joel's bedroom door to ask him to help me *schlep* the boxes upstairs and to let him know that we'd been given a task to do together.

"I guess this makes it official. Rosh Hashanah's really coming soon," he said as we walked down the stairs together.

"Yeah. On one hand, I wish we didn't have to polish the silver every year. But in a way, I suppose it's become a tradition," I said.

"It *is* a family tradition—a *Silver* family tradition! Ha! Get it? I crack myself up, sometimes," Joel guffawed.

Oy.

Joel and I got busy polishing the silver. It soon occurred to me that Jeremy was not around.

"Mom?" I peeked into the dining room where she was now placing the china plates upside down (so that they wouldn't get dusty while they sat out for an entire week) in front of each seat at the table. "Why isn't Jay helping us?"

"Oh, he's busy learning his *haftarah* for the bar mitzvah," Mom said without looking up.

"No he's not," I offered ever-so-helpfully, "He's playing on the computer." I know it's tattling, but it wasn't fair that we had to do all the work while he tricked Mom into thinking he was studying. I felt like poor, unfortunate Cinderella, forced to do all the chores while the evil stepsisters (or, in this case, evil twelve-and-a-half-year-old brother), danced and played and carried on.

"I'm sure he's just on the Ohav Zedek website, going over the stuff he needs to learn," Mom defended him, but I could hear the lack of confidence in her voice. She gently put down the plate she was holding and went over to the office.

"Jeremy Aaron Silver! What do you think you're doing?" Guess I was right.

Jeremy skulked up to his room with a guilt-ridden face. He looked right at me and sneered. How did he know that I was the one who told on him? Well, in any case, it felt good for him to get in trouble once in a while. There's nothing like busting your obnoxious older brother to make your day so much better.

Joel and I decided to each do one part of the job in order to make the work go faster. I wiped the polish on the silverware and he washed it off. It was even sort of fun. I think there were probably much worse jobs that Mom could have given us, like cleaning out the toilets or pulling hair out of the shower drain, for example. I was thinking that maybe Jeremy would get one of those less desirable jobs as payback for fooling Mom.

The phone rang and Mom came into the kitchen to get it, since both my hands and Joel's were wet.

"Hi, Mom. How are you?" she asked in a cheery voice. It could have been either of our grandmothers because she calls them both "Mom."

The mystery grandma said something into the phone that we couldn't hear.

"Oh, right," Mom continued. "I forgot you wanted to do that today. Sure, it won't be a problem. Mark and I will take you."

Mystery solved. It was Grandma Ruth.

"Mhmm . . . Okay, I can ask them. Hold on a minute."

Mom put the phone down and turned to me and Joel.

"Kids, Grandpa isn't feeling well and Grandma wants to go visit Uncle Marvin, Aunt Rose and a few other relatives today. She wants to know if you want to come too."

Joel and I looked at each other with a combination of worry, confusion and general freaking out. Uncle Marvin and Aunt Rose were Dad's uncle and aunt who died a long time ago. Was Grandma going senile at such a young age?

"And she says she wants to tell Great Grandma Pearl all about how big you're all getting and that Jeremy's going to become a bar mitzvah this year."

Okay, now she was really scaring us. Great Grandma Pearl was definitely not with us anymore. I remember going to her funeral when we were really little.

Joel and I must have looked like we just saw a family of ghosts, because Mom looked at us with a hint of concern, or maybe it was confusion, in her face. Neither one of us could speak. I stood there, wide-eyed and frozen. Joel shook his head really fast, like a freshly-bathed dog who wanted every last drop of water off his body.

"Are you sure?" she asked. "It would be nice to keep Grandma Ruth company."

We shook our heads again, too scared to speak. Frankly, I felt a little bit nauseous.

"N-n-n-no thanks," Joel finally was able to speak for the two of us.

Mom looked a little disappointed at us and shook her head while speaking into the phone. "They said they want to stay home. I'll ask Jeremy if he wants to go when I get off the phone. How about if we pick you up around two? All right, see you then."

Okay, I was officially frightened. So much so, that I wiped my hands on a dishtowel and ran upstairs to Jeremy's room. I pounded on the door.

"What?" he bellowed from inside his room.

"I need to talk to you—immediately! It's an emergency!"

"Go away! I know it was you who busted me for being on the computer before."

"*Please* let me in! It's serious!"

After a long, quiet pause, the door swung open.

"What?" He looked really annoyed. I noticed that he had his bar mitzvah folder open and it looked like he either really was doing his work or else he was putting on a good show.

I stepped inside his room and was about to close the door when Joel snuck in to be with us. He closed the door behind him.

"Jay, you won't believe this," I started.

"I have nothing to say to *you*, tattler," he sat down in his chair, put his feet up on his desk, and folded his arms across his chest. "What do you want?" he said, turning to Joel.

"Jay, you really won't believe what we just heard downstairs," Joel began, "Mom just asked us if we wanted to go with her, Dad, and Grandma to visit Uncle Marvin, Aunt Rose, and Great Grandma Pearl."

"Yeah, so?"

"Yeah, so? So they're dead! As in when people say, 'May their memories be for a blessing.' They've passed away. Kicked the bucket. They're in that big fluffy place in the sky. Grandma says she wants to go 'talk' to Great Grandma Pearl. And now they're going to ask you if you want to go, too. Something spooky and extremely weird is going on here. We wanted to warn you." Joel said in a panicky voice. Jay was completely calm.

"Why are you not freaking out? Did you hear what I just told you?"

"Yeah, monkey brains, of course I did, and why would I freak out? They're going to visit the cemetery. They do this every year before Rosh Hashanah. Lots of people do that. Where've you been?"

Joel and I looked at each other in the awkward silence that followed.

"Oh," Joel managed.

"They do?" I croaked.

"Still not talking to *you*," Jay said.

"They do?" Joel repeated on my behalf.

"Every year."

"How did we not know that?" I asked.

"Yeah, how did we not know that?" Joel jumped in, knowing that Jay wasn't going to answer me.

"I guess they never mentioned it to you before because they thought you guys were too little to go to the cemetery until now. And, clearly, you're quite mature and ready to go now," he hissed in a sarcastic tone. It made me glad that I told on him earlier.

"How were we supposed to know?" Joel demanded. "Are you going to go?"

"Nah, I don't think so. I have too much homework and bar mitzvah stuff to do."

Just then, Mom knocked on Jeremy's door. Jeremy took his feet off the desk.

"Jay? May I come in for a second?" she asked.

"Sure," he said so pleasantly you'd think he was running for office or something. Quite a difference from the attitude he was giving me.

"Dad and I are going to take Grandma Ruth to the cemetery today. Will you come with us?"

"I think I'm going to stay home and do my homework and haftarah stuff," he said.

"I'm really glad to hear that you've decided to settle down and do your work now, Jay," Mom said, "But I think you should come with us this year. Now that you're almost a bar mitzvah, you should start taking on more responsibilities. This would be a nice mitzvah for you to do. It would mean a lot to Grandma Ruth."

"But, Mom, it's so creepy there!" Jeremy whined. So much for his pleasant politician act. Now who was being immature?

"It's really not, honey. It's actually quite peaceful. And it's a nice tradition that we do every year. We go, we 'check in' with the family members, and we pay our respects. You're really old enough to be a part of it now."

Jeremy shot a superior look at the two of us as if to say, "Not like you two babies."

"Fine, I'll go," he said reluctantly, "as long as you promise that it won't be too creepy."

"I promise. And thank you. I know that Grandma will appreciate you being there. I'm proud of you for making a good choice." Mom said ruffling his hair as she walked out of the room. Then she popped her head back in and asked, "YaYa and YoYo, are you sure you don't want to go? It would be nice to go as a family."

"Thanks for the invitation, Mom," said Joel, "but I don't think I'm *mature* enough to handle that yet," he glanced sideways at Jeremy, hiding a smirk. "Maybe next year."

"Same here," I chimed in. "Say 'hi' to Great Grandma Pearl for me," I threw in for good measure.

"And you two will be all right staying home alone?"

This spring, Mom started allowing us to stay home without a grown-up in the house, as long as Jeremy was home (as if he'd be any protection if something went wrong). Then, once he went away to sleep-away camp, Joel and I were allowed to stay home on our own as long as we were together.

"We'll be fine, Mom," Joel said reassuringly. "You'll have your phone with you, right?"

"Of course," Mom replied. "Okay then, Jeremy, we'll be leaving in about twenty minutes."

And with that, Mom left the room and closed the door. No more than ten seconds passed when she popped back in and said to me and Joel, "Guys, since you're staying home, I have a few more chores that I need done. I'll give you a list before I leave. Okay? Thanks." The door clicked shut again.

"Classic!" Jeremy hooted.

Funny, I thought to myself. *I still feel like we're getting the better end of the deal.*

Joel and I headed back downstairs to finish polishing the silver, the first of what felt like a thousand pre-holiday tasks that we ended up doing that day.

A Happy New Year

Erev Rosh Hashanah, the evening when the holiday actually starts, finally rolled around. It was almost time to go to Grandma and Grandpa's house for dinner. I was ready before everyone else, so I called Abby to make a plan with her to meet up in the bathroom at shul the next day if services got too long to sit through.

When I got off the phone, I started looking at all the Rosh Hashanah cards we had received that were sitting on top of the mantle. They had pictures of shofars, apples and honey, doves symbolizing peace, and scenes of Jerusalem. While I was looking at them, Joel tapped me on the shoulder and handed me an envelope.

"Here's a Rosh Hashanah card that I made for you," he said.

"You made me a card? That's so nice of you," I said taking it from him and sitting down on the couch to read it.

I tore the envelope open and on the cover it said:

Wishing you a very happy . . .

Then I opened it up and read:

ROACH *Hashanah!* And at that moment, Joel tossed a nasty, disgusting plastic cockroach on my lap.

"EEEEEW, eew, gross, yuck, eew!" was all I kept saying, over and over, as I tossed it off of me. "*That is so gross!* What's *wrong* with you?"

"It was just a joke," Joel said sheepishly. I don't think he expected quite that strong of a reaction.

"I can't believe you did that to me!" I yelled at him, almost in tears. But then, after I got over the shock and repulsiveness of the fake cockroach and I thought about it for a minute, I secretly thought it was kind of a clever play on words. "That was really, really nasty. Why do you have to play jokes on me all the time?" I asked feeling a little bit hurt.

"I really just thought it would make you laugh. I didn't mean to scare you."

I squinted at him, not buying that for a second.

"Okay, maybe I wanted to scare you a little. But in a funny way. I'm really very sorry."

"Promise me you won't do that again,"

"I promise."

"Come on kids, it's time to call Bubby and Zayde," Mom called out, coming into the room. Each year, before we leave the house to go to dinner at Grandma and Grandpa's house, we call Bubby and Zayde to wish them a

Shanah Tovah, a happy new year. It has become a tradition for us to do that on the years that they aren't with us.

Then, just like every year, we walked the nine blocks over to Grandpa Jack and Grandma Ruth's house, dressed up in our nice clothes, "looking spiffy" as Dad likes to say.

I looked up as we walked. The sun was just starting to go down. I looked for the moon but it wasn't dark enough to see it yet. I thought about how cool it was that back in the old times, those rabbis at the Temple in Jerusalem were looking for the exact same moon that I was looking for. I was in the middle of thinking about how amazing it was that, although I couldn't see it yet, I would be looking at the very same moon that people did hundreds, even thousands of years ago, when all of a sudden Jeremy yelled at me, "YaYa, watch where you're going! You almost stepped in that."

Oh man, I hate it when people don't clean up after their dogs. Jeremy really saved me from one huge mess. *Wow*, I thought, *that was the nicest thing that Jeremy has done for me in ages.*

When we got to their house, Grandpa Jack opened the door and we all gave him hugs and wished him a Shanah Tovah. As I stepped into their house, all of my favorite holiday smells came floating toward me and surrounded me. It felt like the holiday itself was wrapping its arms around me and giving me a big hug. I felt warm all over.

I got a whiff of all my favorite foods mixed together: chicken soup with matzah balls, brisket, Grandma's famous sweet noodle *kugel*, honey cake, and *challah*. It all smelled wonderful and my mouth started to water right away. It amazed me that every year it smelled exactly the same. And I loved it.

Everyone was in a good mood. Even cool-guy Jeremy seemed to be pretty relaxed and not annoyed that he had to hang out with his un-cool family.

The doorbell rang; it was Aunt Rachel and Uncle David. Aunt Rachel is Dad's younger sister. Uncle David isn't really our uncle yet, but he will be in two months. They're getting married in November, and Jeremy, Joel, and I are all going to be in the wedding. I've been waiting my whole life to be in a wedding. I'm so excited!

Everyone hugged and kissed and wished one another a happy and healthy New Year. I went into the kitchen to see how Grandma was doing.

"Shanah Tovah, Grandma," I said.

"Hello, sweetheart," Grandma said as she wiped her hands on her apron and came over to give me a big hug.

"It smells so good in here," I said into her armpit. (I didn't actually mean that her armpit smelled good, but she was still hugging me!)

She finally let go of me. "Thank you, YaYa. You're such a sweet girl. You know, you should really come over and learn how to make some of these dishes with me. You're the perfect age to learn how to cook. When I was a little girl—"

"I know, I know," I interrupted, "you were doing all the cooking and shopping by the time you were ten."

"That's right, and it was a good thing, too, because my mother, your great-grandmother, was not exactly what you'd call a gourmet chef," she said.

"You mean like the time she cooked a turkey and forgot to pluck off the feathers and clean out the insides?" I asked.

Grandma showed the slightest hint of a frown. "You mean I told you this already?"

"Maybe once or twice," I said. I didn't want to hurt her feelings. The truth is that I'd heard this story almost every time I'd come into the kitchen to talk with her.

"Did I tell you how she burned a pot of soup once? Whoever heard of burning soup?"

I nodded. I think I've heard all the stories about Great Grandma Pearl. I sort of remember visiting her at The Davidson Residence before she died when I was four. But I feel like I really remember her from all the stories I've heard about her.

"Oy! No kidding? What can I tell you? I'm getting old, YaYa."

"No way, Grandma, you're not old," I said.

"That's why I love you so much, Yael Esther Silver. You keep me young. You know that I love you to pieces, right?"

"Yeah, I know that," I said while picking a crunchy noodle from the kugel sitting on the stovetop and popping it into my mouth. "I also know that I love this kugel."

"All right, so I'll tell you something you don't know. It's time to eat," Grandma said.

Actually, I figured that one out, too. Everyone was here, the food smelled delicious and the table looked beautiful. It was definitely time to get started. Good thing, too, because the food smelled so incredible that I didn't think I could wait another minute to gobble it up.

15

Apples and Honey

The table was set with Grandma's best dishes and fancy glasses on a pretty, white lace tablecloth. There was a large mound hiding under a rainbow-colored cloth that I made when I was in preschool.

I love that Grandma always keeps and uses all the stuff we make for her. Even with all her elegant china dishes and fancy-schmancy crystal glasses, she still puts out the magic-marker-colored challah cover. She always says that the gifts we make for her are more precious than a million diamonds. I knew that the large mound hiding under the cover was really two round loaves of challah. I love challah. It's one of my favorite foods on *Shabbat* and holidays. I knew that Grandma had just baked it in the morning and I couldn't wait to get my hands on it.

Rabbi Green explained the other day that we have a round challah on Rosh Hashanah, instead of a braided one like we do on Shabbat, to remind us that the year is like a circle. It always goes around and never ends; it just starts over again.

He also said that there are lots of different symbols that people use on Rosh Hashanah. Some people even put a fish head on the table because Rosh Hashanah is the head of the year (*rosh* really means "head" in Hebrew). Another one of those funny customs, I guess. I was glad that Grandma didn't put a fish head on the table. I don't think I would have been able to enjoy her delicious gefilte fish while some other fish was looking up at me and making me feel guilty for eating its relative.

Also on the table was a plate that my parents, brothers, and I gave to Grandma and Grandpa for their anniversary a few years ago. On it were slices of apples, with a pot of honey in the middle.

On a small table under the window in the dining room were three sets of candlesticks waiting to be lit. I walked over to the window, pushed the curtains aside and looked out, trying to spot the moon again. I still couldn't find it. I figured it would be so small that I looked for a tiny sliver, almost like a thin piece of thread hanging in the sky. As I searched for the moon, I couldn't help but wonder what the people in ancient Jerusalem would have done if it was a cloudy night.

I moved in closer and leaned my face right up against the window screen. Since the window was open, it let in a cool breeze. I was deep in thought when all of a sudden

Joel popped up right in front of me on the other side of the window.

"Aagh!" I shrieked in total alarm. "What are you doing out there? You scared the daylights out of me!" I screamed, trembling a bit from his little surprise.

"I came out here to look for the new moon. Want to come out and look with me?" he said, carrying on this conversation as if it was totally normal for him to be outside.

"We're going to start soon." I looked around the room. "Well, the grown-ups are all busy schmoozing right now, so I guess I can come out for a minute," I said.

I walked around to the side of the house where Joel was standing. We both looked up at the sky, which was still not very dark yet.

"I don't see anything," I said looking all around. "Usually you can see the moon, even before it gets completely dark out."

"Maybe go check on the other side of the house," Joel suggested.

I checked and came back.

"Nothing yet," I reported.

"How about across the street?"

Once again, I went to look and returned. After that Joel suggested that I look from the back porch, by the front door, and even by the stop sign on the corner.

Finally, I returned one last time, panting a little because I jogged back. I didn't want to get in trouble for being late.

"Can't find it," I said.

"Yeah," he said, "I don't think you're going to find it tonight. I think when it's a new moon, you can't see it at all."

"What do you mean?" I asked.

"I mean that you can't see the new moon on the first night of the cycle. It's a well-known fact. Learned about it on the Discovery Channel."

I stood there, absorbing what had just happened. He sent me all the way around the house and up the block for nothing? Joel ran away from me as fast as he could. I was ready to clobber him! He tricked me again—and on Erev Rosh Hashanah! Oh, he was going to get it!

There I was, standing outside the window, when I heard Joel call to me from inside, "YaYa, let's go! Grandma is getting ready to light the candles."

"Ellie, what are you doing outside?" Mom demanded, standing in the very spot on the other side of the window that I had been standing in not too long ago. "Get in here! We're all waiting for you!"

Joel gave me a big Cheshire Cat grin.

I joined everyone gathered at the table to light the candles. I secretly smacked Joel on his leg and stuck my tongue out at him without anyone noticing. Grandma covered her head, getting ready to do the prayer for the candles and I knew that it was time to transition out of my aggravation with Joel and into the spirit of the holiday. We all stood quietly while Grandma, Aunt Rachel, and Mom circled the flames three times with their hands and covered their eyes. I looked at the scene in front of me and loved the feeling of having everyone together in one room, although I did wish that Bubby and Zayde could have been there with us too.

All of my senses were filled with the holiday: the mixture of the sweet smells, the sight of the glowing candles, the sound of our voices blending together as we sang the blessing over the candles.

We all found our spots at the dining room table. Grandpa led us in the blessings over the wine and the challah. Then it was time to dip the apples in honey. Even though I love apples and I love honey, and I could easily make that as a snack for myself all year long, I never eat those two things together except on Rosh Hashanah. And when I taste it for the first time each year at the dinner at Grandma and Grandpa's house, it's almost magical.

This is one of my favorite things that we do on Rosh Hashanah. It's a very well-known custom, not just a Silver family tradition. We do it to say that we should have a sweet year. After we passed the apples and honey plate around to everyone at the table, we all said the blessing over eating fruit. Then we said the *Shehechiyanu* prayer to thank God for letting us live to see this moment in time: "*Baruch atah*

Adonai, Eloheinu melech ha'olam, shehecheyanu, v'kiy'manu, v'higiyanu, lazman hazeh. We praise you God, ruler of the universe, for sustaining us and enabling us to reach this season," we all said together.

Grandpa said an extra loud, "Amen!" We all laughed at his gusto.

While everyone at the table was biting into their apple slices, it was time, like every year, for Aunt Rachel to share her favorite Rosh Hashanah memory.

"I think it's time to recall the time my big brother went to dip his apple in the honey." She stood up as if leading an orchestra.

"Was he paying attention when he dipped his apple?" she asked.

"No!" everyone answered in chorus.

"And what, exactly, did he dip his apple in?"

"The horseradish!" we all answered, some of us starting to giggle a little.

"Did he dip it lightly or scoop out a whole bunch?"

"He scooped a whole bunch!" More chuckles.

"Was it Grandpa Jack's homemade, super-hot and spicy horseradish?"

"Yes!"

"And did he eat it?"

"Yes!"

"And what happened next?"

"He poured a whole glass of water on his head because he thought he was on fire!"

Everyone laughed and clapped at the end of the story. Even though the telling of the "Honey/Horseradish Story" has become part of our holiday ritual, we still laugh. We know the punch line, and yet it never stops being funny. Dad went over to Aunt Rachel and gave her a light punch on the shoulder. She swatted him with her hand and then they hugged.

"Rach, you're nothing but trouble. You're lucky I still like you, kiddo," Dad said to his little sister.

Aunt Rachel loves to tease Dad the way Joel teases me. I guess it runs in the family. I think it's funny that when Dad and Aunt Rachel get together, it's like they forget that they're adults and they act like little kids. I wonder if I'll be that way with my brothers when we're grown-ups .

I dipped my apple and let some honey dribble into my mouth before I took a bite. (And yes, I checked to make sure that it wasn't horseradish first!) The sweet taste of the honey mixed with the tart flavor of the apple in my mouth. "Mmmmm," I said out loud. At the same time, I thought to myself, *I don't need a new moon, a fish head or a swinging chicken. For me, this is how I know it's Rosh Hashanah.*

Dinner began and it was just as delicious as it smelled. Everyone was chatting at once. Aunt Rachel was talking excitedly with Mom about the wedding, which seemed, she said, to be coming up faster than she was ready for because she still had so much to do. Even though she was all the way at the other end of the table I could hear them talking about place cards and centerpieces. More details than I needed. I tuned out of that conversation.

I looked over and saw Jeremy actually having a conversation with Uncle David. I wondered what they could possibly be talking about. I tried to imagine Uncle David on a skateboard and couldn't do it. I tried to imagine him playing video games, but that didn't work either. I leaned in closer and was stunned to hear them talking about something really strange—I think it was Israeli politics. Shocking! I giggled to myself as I thought that maybe it was Jeremy, not me, who had been replaced by an alien or a troll or something.

I looked around the table and got a warm feeling all over. When I was done eating, I went up to Grandpa, who was sitting at the head of the table. I leaned over to hug him and his white mustache tickled my cheek. I smelled his cologne as he put his arms around me and kissed me on top of my head. I closed my eyes and took it all in. I realized then that I loved everything about this holiday: the food, my family, the traditions, even the opportunity to hear Uncle David and Jeremy arguing about the Likud Party (whatever that was).

I wouldn't have missed it for the world. Not even Splash World.

16

The Book of Life

The next day we all woke up and got dressed in our new shul outfits. Every year Mom buys us new clothes to wear for Rosh Hashanah. Dad and the boys wore suits. Joel wore a tie with Winnie the Pooh on it. When I pointed at it, he simply shrugged his shoulders and said, "It's the honey holiday." Leave it to Joel the joker.

I wore a long-sleeved blue dress with tiny white flowers all over it. The only problem was that it was meant for the fall and the thermometer on our deck said that it was already seventy-five degrees outside. I was sweating. I looked at Mom and thought that she looked really nice, but I was guessing that she was warm in her outfit, too. She wore a pretty red suit and her favorite hat. Not too many women wear hats at our shul, but Mom loves the way they look, so she wears one to services fairly often. She has quite a collection in her closet. When I was little, I used to love to go in there, take out her hat boxes, and play dress-up in the mirror.

When I complained to Mom about how uncomfortable I was in my dress, she said, "Every year they put the air conditioning on so high that you feel like you're sitting in a meat locker. Trust me, you'll thank me later."

We left our house and walked to synagogue together. I love our neighborhood because we have everything so close by. We can walk to our shul, our grandparents' house and even some stores and restaurants. We also have three different parks we can go to. One is a little too far to walk to, but Dad said that next spring, Joel and I could ride our bikes there on our own as long as we stay on the bike path. That will be really cool!

As we walked along the sidewalk, we ran into other neighbors who were on their way to Rosh Hashanah services. People wished each other a Happy New Year as they passed. Some were walking in our direction and some were going in the opposite direction, toward Ahavas Yisroel.

When we got to shul, Joel went to the kids' service, which is open to kids up until sixth grade. Since the seventh-graders are either just about to be or have already become a bar or bat mitzvah, they are included in the teen service. I think Jeremy was really excited to finally be old enough to go to there. I chose to stay and sit with my family in the big sanctuary. I always love to hear the cantor sing all the melodies that we only get to hear once a year. It really puts me in the mood of the holiday.

I was especially excited to hear the shofar. True, I did hear the shofar that crazy day in class when Rabbi Green stood on his desk and blew it. And in a way I heard it again in my dream when it turned out to be my alarm clock. But there's something special about hearing it for real in synagogue during services.

I was having a good time at first, but after a while, to be totally honest, I started to get a little bored. I wished that I had a good book to read or something. I decided to try to entertain myself. I stared at the back of the seat in front of me and attempted to find designs in the lines of the wood. First, with a bit of imagination, I saw a design that looked a little bit like a teacup. Then I found one that looked like a flower. Next, I spotted a design that looked like a spider. It moved. It was a real spider! Yuck! Before I knew it, it had crawled under the seat in front of me. Well, that was weird.

I started to count the pages in the prayer book. I looked around and checked out the backs of people's heads. I counted the number of people wearing a black kippah versus a blue one. Then I found the fringes of Grandpa Jack's *tallit*, his prayer shawl. I wrapped the fringes around my fingers. I knotted them. I braided them. I tickled my palm with them. I put them up to my mouth and made a mustache with them.

Mom looked over at me and gave me one of her looks: the one that means, "Stop it right now, young lady!" She didn't have to say a word to get that message across.

Grandpa just chuckled and whispered, "I think you look better with a clean shave anyway."

I put the fringes down and tried to figure out what to do with myself next. I looked up at the *bimah* and saw Rabbi Green. He was dressed in a white robe called a *kittel* and so was Cantor Grossman. Rabbi Green's eyes met mine and he smiled at me. I waved back to him. Seeing him made me think about the stuff we talked about in class. I remembered him telling us that we get two days to really stop and think about things. I figured this was as good a time as any; besides, I had nothing else to do. There were no good songs being sung just then, and there seemed to be just a lot of mumbling going on around me.

I thought about what Joel had taught me about t'shuvah. He said we're supposed to try and do better with ourselves, with others and with God.

How could I do better with myself? I wondered. That one came pretty easily to me. I really liked how it felt the other day when I woke up early to a clean, neat bedroom. I liked having time for breakfast and not rushing to the bus stop. I even liked not having to do my homework on the bus and having time to read a good book instead. And I loved being able to keep track of all my things. At that moment I promised myself that I would really try hard to do better with all that organization stuff. My fourth grade teacher, Ms. Holmes, would be proud. Okay, check off number one on my list.

Next I had to figure out who deserved an apology for anything I might have done to them. That one came pretty quickly to me as well. I wasn't always as nice to Joel as I could be. I really don't have to call him Little Bro all the time, especially when I know he doesn't like it. But it is kind of fun to bug him. Okay, okay, I told myself. I'll apologize to Joel for not always being as nice to him as I could be. I'll try to do better in the future. And I'll also try to deal better with Jeremy and his new "cool" attitude. Hopefully it really is just a phase, as Mom said, and he'll get over it soon. Okay, check another one off the list.

My thoughts were interrupted when everyone stood up all at once. I looked up and saw that the ark was being opened. I could see all the Torah scrolls. They were dressed in white, just like the rabbi and the cantor.

Everything looked so light, bright, and fresh. I remembered how Rabbi Green explained that tradition. It's because we are cleaning out our souls and starting the year untarnished and pure. He said that it is kind of like a fresh, clean sheet of paper that would be written on throughout the year. Just like on the first day of school when we open up our brand new notebooks. They're stark white and just waiting to be filled up.

Looking up at the bimah and seeing all that white reminded me of heaven and angels floating around in the clouds. It was just another thing that added to the spirit of the holiday for me.

And then everyone started to sing the prayer *Avinu Malkeinu*. That is definitely one of my favorite Rosh Hashanah melodies. The tune is beautiful but it's also a little bit haunting. And just like the apples and honey that we only eat once a year, we only hear this melody at this time of the year. It really makes it special.

While I was standing there, my mind sort of drifted off and I pictured Corey McDonald singing Avinu Malkeinu. I imagined him standing in front of a microphone swaying and singing sort of a rock 'n' roll version of it. I could see him with his long dark blond bangs in his eyes, wearing a leather jacket and ripped up jeans, really getting into it and rocking out. Then I gave him a costume change and pictured him in a white kittel like Rabbi Green was wearing. (And what do you know? He still looked cute.) I giggled quietly to myself but kept it silent. I couldn't risk another one of Mom's killer looks.

When they closed the ark and we sat down, I started to think about the words to Avinu Malkeinu, which was translated from the Hebrew in the prayer book as "Our Father Our King." I liked how it described God as both a parent we can be close to, who takes care of us and who we can talk to, and then also as someone powerful who is in charge from far away. I decided it was time to work on t'shuvah category number three. I began to wonder how I let God down and what I needed to do better. That one did not come quickly to me. I really didn't know how to answer that question. The good news was that I had another whole day to think about it. *Good thing Rosh Hashanah lasts for two days*, I thought to myself, kind of laughing. I wondered if Joel had the time to think about this stuff, too. I decided that I didn't have to do this alone and that I could ask him what he thought about it when we got home.

I asked Mom if I could go to the bathroom. She looked at her watch and said, "I was wondering how long it would take you to ask." Everyone knows that the kids end up in the hall or the bathroom at some point, and I was no different. There's only so long you can sit there. I was hoping that Abby remembered our plan and that she'd meet me in the bathroom.

"Go ahead," Mom told me. "Just don't stay in there too long. You should either be in here with us or at the kids' service, not hanging out in the bathroom." I made a phony face like I was shocked and appalled that she would even think that I'd hang out in the bathroom. I love kidding around with her.

"I was a kid once too, YaYa, and it wasn't as long ago as you may think. I know all about the bathroom routine. Go and come back soon."

"Thanks," I whispered. I kissed her on the cheek. I think she's a pretty cool mom.

I escaped to the bathroom. Abby was not waiting for me by the door as we had talked about, so I went inside. I noticed how clean and sparkly the toilet was and realized that someone actually had to clean it. It was very white and shiny. I had never really paid attention to that before. As the water swirled around, it reminded me of the splashy, twisty water slides at Splash World.

I walked over to the sink to wash my hands and watched the water flow out of the faucet. I played with the warm water as it ran through my fingers. Splash. Splash. Splash. It made me think about Splash World even more.

I surprised myself when I realized that while I was still quite disappointed that I wasn't able to go to Splash World, at least I wasn't as sad about it as I had been before. I understood that while it seemed like it was the chance of a lifetime, in reality, it wasn't. Splash World would be there next week and the week after that and the one after that. Rosh Hashanah wouldn't be back for another year. *Hopefully, I'll get there somehow between now and next Rosh Hashanah,* I thought to myself.

Abby never came into the bathroom, so I left to go see if anyone else was hanging around. No one was in the hallway. Or in the lobby. Or in the stairway. Or in the other bathroom at the far end of the building. Or even in the front entryway. Where was everyone? That was weird.

Usually kids were swarming all over the place. I thought for sure I'd find at least one friend to hang out with. I did see some older kids and some young moms gathering in the lobby. The moms were chatting while nursing their babies or chasing after their toddlers (one mom was doing both at the same time!) but I couldn't find anyone that I wanted to hang out with. I figured that Abby changed her mind and went to the kids' service after all. Maybe the kids' service turned out to be so good this year that everyone was in there. Even still, I wanted to stay with my family in the big service.

With nothing exciting going on, and no one to play with, I dragged myself back to the sanctuary. Aunt Rachel and Uncle David had arrived while I was gone. I squeezed in between Grandpa and Uncle David. Not long after I sat down it was time to stand up again—that happens a lot in services.

This time the ark was opened for another haunting tune. Cantor Grossman sang, *"B'rosh hashanah yikateivun, uv'yom tzom kippur yeichateimun."* I took a look at the English translation on the opposite page, "On Rosh Hashanah it is written and on Yom Kippur it is sealed. Who will live and who will die. Who will be born and who will perish."

I felt a chill run up and down my back. It was a little bit creepy to think about what could happen within the next year. It freaked me out to think that in one year, next Rosh

Hashanah, things could be so different. Good or bad, it might not—and probably would not—be the same.

First of all, Aunt Rachel and Uncle David were going to get married. Aunt Rachel had mentioned that she and Uncle David wanted to start a family right away after they got married. After all, as her older brother (a.k.a. my dad) so politely put it, "She's no spring chicken." Maybe there would be a baby in the family next year. Maybe they'd have twins, too, and there would be two new cousins! (Maybe we could call them GaGa and GoGo?) Or maybe someone would die. I did not want to think about that.

The story that I've learned is that God sits in front of a big open book and writes down the name of every person who will live this coming year. I'm still not sure whether I believe in this whole "Book of Life" story. I am sure, though, that I felt like I had no control over what was going to happen this year. From what I've heard, that was up to God.

Except, of course, for the things I could control, like being more organized and nicer to Joel. Maybe, I thought, if I tried harder to do better, I could make my life a little better, even if I couldn't be in charge of everything that happens. Maybe I could even help make someone else's life nicer and better, too.

Time to sit down again.

As I sat there I sort of appreciated the fact that I have teachers, parents, and a tradition that required me to be here for two days. I realized that this year, unlike past years, I was starting to understand what Rosh Hashanah was all about, and I was getting more out of being in synagogue than just playing around with my friends and sitting with my family. I also realized that Mom was right: it was freezing in shul! Even in my long-sleeved dress, my teeth were chattering. I cuddled up next to Grandpa and wrapped myself inside his tallit. As I sat there, soaking up his warmth, I closed my eyes and thought about how glad I was that I had the time to think, to hear all the melodies that I love, and to be with my family.

I still wanted to get to Splash World and hoped that someday I would, but this was where I needed to be and where I wanted to be.

I was sliding into the New Year and I couldn't be happier!

T'shuvah in a Shoebox

After services were over, I decided to talk to Joel about all the stuff I thought about in synagogue. We walked home together, talking, and continued at our house. Even after we were done I still wasn't sure about the whole God piece of my t'shuvah, but I did come up with an idea for apologizing to Joel.

I took an old shoebox that I had in my closet and inside it, I put a photo of the two of us when we were babies. I found him in the kitchen having a snack of challah with honey (another one of my favorite things to eat on Rosh Hashanah). I put the shoebox on the table in front of him.

"What's this?" Joel asked.

"A shoebox," I said.

"Duh. I know it's a shoebox, YaYa. Why did you put it here?"

"Open it," I said and slid it closer to him.

Joel opened it up and took out the picture. He looked at it and smiled. It was a snapshot of the two of us splashing around in a little kiddie pool when we were about one and a half. Joel was holding a red Popsicle over his head. We were both laughing. I think we both found it absolutely hysterical. He was a joker even back then. It was such a fun picture that you couldn't look at it and not smile.

"I decided to do a 'Shoebox of T'shuvah.' I want you to know that even though I haven't always been as nice to you as I could be, I really like being your twin sister. And even though I am *much* older than you," I paused and cleared my throat for effect, "I will stop calling you Little Bro since I know you really don't like it. I will try to be nicer to you this year. Also, I will try to laugh at your jokes a little more." Then I thought for a moment. "That might be the hardest one of all to keep."

"Ha ha," Joel said. "I thought you were going to be nicer to me."

"Oops," I said. "Okay, starting . . . now!"

"Well, I guess I could try to be nicer to you, too." Joel smirked. "And maybe I'll even tease you less about Corey McGriddles."

I put one hand on my hip and shook a fist at him.

"Starting . . . now!" he said. We both laughed.

Mom and Dad walked in and asked what we were doing. I explained to them how I thought Rabbi Green was talking about shoeboxes when he was really talking about t'shuvah. Then we told them about my idea for a t'shuvah shoebox. Mom whispered something to Dad and he nodded.

"May I borrow your shoebox, YaYa?" Mom asked.

"Sure, go ahead," I said, kind of puzzled.

A minute later she walked back with the shoebox in her hand.

"Here you go, YaYa. This is Dad's and my box of t'shuvah." She glanced sideways at Dad and smiled.

I took the box but didn't stop looking at Mom. Jeremy walked into the kitchen then, too. He picked up an apple, took a bite (heaven forbid he should miss an opportunity to eat), and said with his mouth full of apple, "Hey, guys. What's up?"

"Mom is giving YaYa a t'shuvah box," Joel said.

"A tissue box? Why, does she have a cold or something?" Jeremy asked.

"No, it's a t'shuvah box," Joel repeated.

"A shoebox? Why would she need a shoebox if she has a cold?" Jeremy asked, looking completely confused.

"It's a shoebox with something inside that represents t'shuvah, how she and Dad want to improve themselves this year. Nobody has a cold. But it is a way to try to make yourself better. It's a Rosh Hashanah thing."

"Alrighty then," Jeremy said, sort of rolling his eyes. But I noticed that he didn't leave. He was just as curious as the rest of us.

I opened the box. Inside was a colorful brochure. It was from Splash World. I looked up at Mom even more puzzled than before.

"We want to try to relax a bit and have some fun with you guys. We know how much you've been wanting to go to Splash World and that you were pretty disappointed when you couldn't go with Megan."

"Yeah, I was, but I'm pretty much over that now."

"Well," she paused and looked at me and then at Joel and then at Jeremy, "In honor of your birthday next month, Dad and I are taking all three of you to Splash World to celebrate."

"Cool!" Jeremy blurted out.

"Oh my gosh, you guys are the best!" I screamed. I hugged her and then Dad.

Joel got very quiet and looked down at the table.

"Don't worry, YoYo," Mom said, "we'll still take you to the Science Center or the batting cages if that's where you'd like to go for your birthday. Plus, they have tons of other things to do at Splash World besides the slides. They have a whole section of water games and an arcade as well. I visited their website. It looks great and I think you'll like it a lot."

"Thanks, Mom," Joel said. Then he added with a sly grin, "Are you guys going to try the slides?"

"Don't push it, YoYo," Mom said. We all laughed.

"Tell you what," Dad said to Joel, "I'll go down the slides if you will."

"No way! I'm sticking to the arcade."

Just then Jeremy picked up the shoebox and disappeared from the kitchen with it. I heard his big feet thud up the stairs and the door to his bedroom close. I wondered what he was going to do. Was it possible that he was going to "clean out his soul" like the rest of us?

I had a feeling that we just started a new Silver family tradition.

Acknowledgements

Not only does it take a village to raise a child, it also takes a village to publish a book. I would like to thank my family for all of their encouragement and support in writing this book. I love you all. To my friends, relatives, and all the kids who read my manuscript and shared opinions: Thank you for taking part in this journey with me. You've all helped me, in one way or another, and I'm so grateful!

To my amazing husband, Gary: Thank you for nudging me when I needed that extra little push. I couldn't have done this without your encouragement, enthusiasm, and love.

To my children, Ari, Ilana, and Eitan, who have grown up over the past few years with YaYa and YoYo: Thanks for being my cheerleaders! You are my biggest inspiration. And thanks for welcoming a bunch of fictional characters into our lives and into our home.

To Sheyna Galyan at Yaldah Publishing: Thank you for the best email I've ever received, which opened with: "I read your manuscript and I WANT IT!" I'm eternally grateful to you for accepting my work and for helping me to become a published author.

To my editor, Leslie Martin: Thank you for your editing expertise. You are so insightful. It has been a pleasure meeting you all around town to work on the manuscript. Next cup of coffee is on me!

To the students and teachers at the Amos and Celia Heilicher Minneapolis Jewish Day School: Thank you for welcoming me into your classrooms to share my story and to give me feedback so that I could tighten up my writing. I have learned so much from my visits with you and I hope you enjoyed the process as well as the end result.

To the clergy at Beth El Synagogue in Saint Louis Park, Minnesota: Thank you for your guidance and wisdom, which have helped me in writing this book and beyond.

To all fans of *YaYa & YoYo*: Stay tuned—*Shaking in the Shack* (Book 2) is on its way!

About the Author

Dori Weinstein grew up in Queens, New York. She is a graduate of Binghamton University and Teachers College, Columbia University. Dori taught in public schools in New York City as well as the Talmud Torah Jewish Day School in St. Paul, Minnesota. She currently teaches Hebrew to preschoolers. She lives in Minneapolis with her husband and their three children, all of whom love water parks (except for Dori!). Visit Dori on Facebook, Twitter, her blog at doriweinstein.blogspot.com, and on the web at yayayoyo.com.